Liquid Lust

E. L. Lamont

Ink Think
— A PUBLISHING CO. —

First paperback edition March 2021

Cover and book design by Devon L. Jackson

ISBN 978-1-950127-05-4 (paperback)

www.inkthinkpress.com

Table of Contents

Table of Contents

Time

He was running late, something he hated with a passion. He searched around the bed for his keys, cursing himself for not putting them on the dresser as he always did. His phone was buzzing off the hook and he knew it was his assistant wondering where the hell he was. If he could just find his damn keys...and his underwear.

"All this running around," a voice muttered sleepily from under the rumpled covers.

"I aint say nothing about all that running you was doing last night," he called back, dropping to his knees to check under the chair and nightstand.

"Um, as I recall, you did. In fact, I remember several rather colorful, explicit, and might I add, downright mean things you said."

"I'm sorry. Did I hurt your feelings?" He pumped his fist in triumph as he found his keys curled around one leg of the distant ottoman. How the hell did they end up there and like that?

"A little bit, yes. Of course, you could make it up to me."

"Uh huh," he called back, distant, eyes and mind still trying to locate his missing items of clothing. He did NOT go commando; two bad experiences with a zipper as a kid and he almost teared up every time he even thought the word. "And how's that?"

She flipped back the covers and stretched like a cat.

"You could come hurt this pussy."

Ok. That threw him. She laughed as she watched his features change as his brain reset.

"You gotta stop saying shit like that. You know it fucks with my mental."

"Oh, is it your mental it fucks with? And here I thought it was your head." For emphasis, she smiled and reached for his dick.

"Aye, woman! Stop that! You know I'm running

3

behind."

She turned around and arched her back.

"You said something about 'behind'?"

He groaned and rolled his eyes heavenward.

"Why are you doing this to me?"

"Because I'm evil." She laughed, deep and throaty and with genuine good humor. For all her teasing and flaunting and mischievousness, she was really a good and solid woman. Not for the first time he realized just how amazing that was — and dangerous.

"Look, you know I've got this meeting about the merger. You know there's several mil on the line. You know that if I'm not there the board will flip because COO's kinda need to be involved in this kinda stuff."

"And I also know how much you love watching me lick my cum off your dick." Looking over her shoulder, she slid two fingers into herself as he watched, slow and deep, making sure he caught each movement. "So…"

He groaned again, falling to his knees at the edge of the bed. Damn his weakness! And his dick.

"Why do you always insist on doing this to me," he asked as he placed his face between her thick chocolate thighs and placed the first lick against her fatness. She purred and arched further, body sinking into the deep plushness of the bed while her pussy sunk into the deep plushness of his lips.

"Because you always insist on doing me like you do. Aint nobody told you to fuck me like that."

"As I recall," he mumbled, lips full of hers, "that's actually precisely what you told me."

"Shit, I didn't know you'd actually do it. Most niggas…" She stopped, shuddering, her breath caught in her throat as he brought her to her first orgasm. He lapped her up, then chided her with mock sternness.

"Now what did I tell you about comparing me to other niggas?" She arched her back again as his tongue dipped deep between her lips.

"You said aint no other niggas like you."

"Precisely. And?"

"Baby, you aint never lied."

He laughed and smacked her ample ass.

"Why you sound like somebody's auntie just now?"

She spread her legs and raised her ass higher.

"Baby, you could make me somebody's mama right now. Gaht damn, I need you to fuck me."

"I'm sorry, what?"

She looked back over her shoulder, soft blonde dreads trailing across her perfectly smooth hershey-colored back. Her eyes had the slightest hints of hazel, like gold flecks trapped in molasses. He loved her eyes, the way they looked at him, at the world, saw all and everything, its reality and value and beauty. He liked that he could look at her and see his reflection, not in vanity, but rather, in truth. He looked at her and saw a reflection of himself, a woman as strong and

6

confident and ambitious and determined and committed as he was. He looked at her and saw love — and then she licked her lips and he instantly saw pure, unadulterated lust.

He stood up and unbuttoned his shirt. She laughed gleefully and scooted back to the edge of the bed. He placed his hands on her hips, smoothing the soft flesh, loving its warmth and pliability and weight.

He was bout to beat the brakes off this ass.

"Again, I think I must have misheard. You want me to do what?"

"Fuck me. Fuck me, daddy. Fuck me til this pussy cums for you."

"You say that like it's an option." He laughed, kneading the small of her back while she flexed and writhed beneath him.

"You know what I mean."

"Mayhaps." He traced his fingernails down the cleft of her spine, a move that always made her shudder. He looked between her legs and saw a long silver line descending from her lips to the sheets beneath. She was so wet she literally dripped. He caught his breath as his dick jumped like a trip hammer. For just a moment, he felt his ironclad control begin to slip, but caught himself. See, most niggas lacked control, lacked the power over self that created the best lovers. They rushed and rammed and rode with reckless abandon, feeding their own frenzy of lust to get to that nut, and therefore left their partners empty and unsatisfied. It was a common malady, bemoaned by women the world over. Until they met him. For he was a gaht damned unicorn, a man that loved well because he listened well and therefore learned well. And what he loved most was loving beautiful women. He listened to their dreams and their screams with equal facility. He learned their mannerisms and their moans and knew how to enhance each. He fucked them as they wanted to be fucked. No, scratch that. He fucked them as they NEEDED to be fucked, and that because he truly, truly

8

enjoyed giving them that pleasure. He was the ultimate giving lover because giving gave back to him. Their moans were his own, their screams erupted into his lungs, their shades and shudders translated into his flesh and feelings and he was baptized and reborn in them. He fucked them as they needed to be fucked — and oh, how they returned the favor.

"Mayhaps," he said again, grabbing handfuls of her chocolate flesh. "Tell me," he asked as he slipped himself inside her, a move that drew forth a long, shuddering sigh, "what's our record so far?" She collapsed back on the bed, wriggling her hips back and against him.

"From fucking or head?"

"Either." He glided in and out of her slowly and steadily, allowing them both to acclimate to the sensation, the warmth, the expectation.

"Nine for head, seven for fucking."

"Hmmm," he muttered, feigning disappointment. "Is that all?"

9

"Is that all? Damn, nigga, you tryna kill a bitch?" She screamed as he plunged into her unexpectedly, hard, deep and long.

"You said hurt this pussy."

If he'd expected a response, he'd have been disappointed. However, he didn't, so wasn't, because he knew she'd now lost all ability to speak. See, they'd danced this dance before and he knew just how to lead. Crossing his hands over her hips, he subtly shifted her position, raising her ass just so so that he could find that one spot she loved. He was rewarded by a near ear-splitting scream.

"Gotcha, bitch," he laughed to himself.

Her pussy creamed all over his dick, so slick that even for all its grip and all his thickness, it was becoming a smooth proposition. So he leaned forward, placed his knees inside hers to spread them further, put his hands on her shoulders to both steady himself and to lock her in place, and went to work.

And when I say "work," I mean WORK. He

slammed into her with practiced, calculated force, not the wild, reckless, ferocity most niggas employ when they *think* they fucking. No, this was the force that came from knowledge of bodies in motion, of weight and counterweight, of loads and bearing. This was a master at his craft, calculating inches of depth and girth against angles and organs. This was knowing just how far she could comfortably curve her spine, and then angling against that edge so that she felt it shock through her entire body. This was knowing just how hard she could throw it back and so knowing how far beyond that to throw it to her to elicit the right response. In short, this was FUCKIN fuckin. And he was on a mission.

He suddenly slowed, leaning back slightly onto his heels. She shuddered, taking a breath, five orgasms in and tingly. She thought that maybe he was kidding about the record, just talking shit because he loved to talk shit. Shit, she was satisfied already; completely, thoroughly, immensely satisfied. Yeah, she'd give him some hell for "quitting early," but they'd both know it was a ruse. She was just about to turn to say something jokingly spiteful when he grabbed a fistful of her hair and rammed into her again. Her mouth gaped wide as her pussy slammed shut around his dick. She immediately came again, not even thinking it was possible. "Gaht damn!" she thought in the part of her mind still capable of coherency. "What the entire fuck IS this nigga?"

"Oh-ho, you thought we were done, huh?" He laughed, his voice deep and resonant, and she could feel it vibrating through her body. "Nah, bitch, you said you wanted this work, even got me late for work, so I'ma work this shit out on you."

One hand locked in her hair, the other around her waist, he pulled her into him as he pounded her relentlessly. Alternating rhythms, angles, rotations of his hips, he found and fucked every spot she knew and a dozen others she didn't. His hands were ever moving, now in her hair, now on her hips, now on her tits and her clit, now around her throat. She felt like she was being fucked by an anaconda or one of those hentai monsters. She laughed, suddenly, at the thought.

At this point he had her upright, back against his chest, ass on his thighs, pussy wrapped firmly and wetly around his throbbing thickness. One hand massaged her belly as the other played with her breasts, tweaking her nipples. His head was on her shoulder, lips nuzzling into the nape of her neck. She could feel his breath against her heartbeat and it felt like beauty.

"What's so funny?" he asked, nipping lightly at her sweaty, chocolate skin.

"I was just thinking that I know what them anime bitches be going through. Nigga, you got mo appendages than an octopus." They laughed together, then, thrilling as the action translated to their loins, he thumping and throbbing inside her, she gripping and pulsating around him.

"Aye, talk nerdy to me, baby." They laughed again as he kissed her earlobe and then turned her face toward his. He looked into her eyes as he kissed her lips, savoring the warmth and fire in both.

"So," he said, still holding her to him as they rocked gently, slow and sweet now, wrapped in each other in more ways than one. "How many we up to now?"

"Shit, I lost count somewhere around twelve." She moaned as he pushed her forward again, already increasing his rhythm.

"Well, guess I won't be making that meeting today..."

Cry Baby

So I decide to surprise you today at work. I was in the area, had a taste for something spicy and sweet, and smiled when I thought where that would lead.

I had you on the phone, telling me about your day, the people perennially pissing you off, the coworker you wanted to strangle, the boss who just didn't have a clue, and just as you exit the elevator with a perfectly formed curse word on your perfectly formed lips, you see me smiling into your eyes. You laugh at my deception — then smirk as you see my growing erection. Hey, what can I say; you've got that effect on me. You come close to give me a hug — and to slide my length in the gap between your legs.

"What are you doing here," you say at my neck.

"Was in the neighborhood and thought we could catch lunch," I reply, a sparkle of innocence in my eye.

"Oh, what did you have in mind?"

My smile is all the answer you need.

"Me, then."

"Well," I laugh, "I thought you might want some tube steak as well."

You laugh and grab my hand, pulling me along the halls. A while back you found an out-of-the-way office on a largely empty floor that was both big enough and remote enough to provide the privacy we need for our "lunch breaks." You're pulling me along, almost running in your haste to get a taste of what you've been craving.

"Slow down, mama. We don't wanna arouse suspicion."

"Speaking of arousal," you say as you stop, turn, and shove your tongue down my throat.

"Well damn," I gasp, dick thumping like a well-tuned Chevy. "Fuck suspicion, we can do it right here."

You laugh and go back to hauling me along. Up the side stairs, down a long row of empty cubicles and into a quiet, corner office. It's a small conference room, left over from some firm that had occupied the floor but moved on when the contract or the talent ran out. Large windows overlook the city below, though they are smoky with tint and hung with long, wooden blinds. A buffet for drinks, a few soft chairs, and the pièce de résistance: a long, oak conference table. I laugh when we enter.

"What," you say turning into me again, rubbing your body against mine like a cat that's been missing its owner all day.

"I think I can still see your ass-print from last time." You push me away.

"Mine or yours?"

"Hey, you saying I got a fat ass?"

"Not as fat as that dick."

I bite my lip in anticipation. The time for talk has passed; now it's time for straight fuckin.

17

You nuzzle at my neck as I unzip your sweater. You grab my hair as I pull the top of your dress to the side and begin to nibble on your nipples. And when my hands slide your dress up your thighs and cup that thick, round ass, you let out a moan that I'm sure they can hear a floor away.

"Daddy," you breathe as my hands knead and squeeze, my tongue playing tricks on your breasts. "Daddy," you say again, "I'm so fucking wet."

"Really?" I ask, looking into your eyes, a smile on my lips. "Show me."

You reach down between us and slide your hand down the front of your boy shorts. A moan escapes your lips and a shudder racks your body — and then you reach back up and place your fingers between my lips.

"See," you breathe, and my eyes glaze over with lust. I push you back on the table, throw your dress up around your hips and rip your shorts off. You pull your legs back and grab handfuls of my hair as I

18

run my tongue along the insides of your thighs. I'm savoring the sight of that peach, that sweet, fuzzy fruit that's calling my name even now.

"Daddy," you moan again, "please."

"Please what," I mumble into the inside of your thigh.

"Do it."

"Do what," I speak into the crease between leg and mound.

"Eat me."

"Say it again," I say as I place a light kiss on your nether lips.

"Eat me," you say again, louder, and my lips part yours and come to rest on the slickness inside.

"Again."

"Eat me, please. Fucking eat me!" Your fingers spasm in my hair, your back arches, legs clench, body trembling already.

"If you insist," I say and then proceed to fulfill your request. My tongue dips in and out of your lips, flicking against the wet, steamy inside of your cunt, around and down, back and forth, again and again. When you feel my tongue slip inside you, you moan. When you feel my nose brush your clit, you shudder. But when my lips wrap gently around your pearl, pulling it into my mouth and my tongue begins to dance circles against it, you arch your back and scream.

"Yes! Yes! Yes! Please! Right there! Dear, God; right there!"

Your thighs clench my head, your hands pull my hair, your ass beats against the wood of the table. You shudder and shake and cover my face in your lust as my lips and tongue take you through climax after climax. As the last aftershocks rumble through your frame, your breath slows, and your hands relax in my hair. You stretch lazily, and appreciatively — until you feel me slide into you. You gasp and immediately begin to clench and spasm on my dick.

"Oh, you thought this was a meal for one?"

You try to answer but you can't find the air to speak.

"Oh, were you going to say something?" You look at me in silent accusation, your body writhing as you take my thrusts again and again. I grab your legs and push them up to your chest and take one long, thick, slow stroke into you.

"I can't quite hear you."

"*Fuck me, you big-dicked bastard.*"

This is not screamed, not sighed, not whispered. It is a command. You look in my eyes and I see that look that drives me fucking crazy, that mixture of violence and lust that signals an epic sex session.

"Well, damn. How can I say no to that?" And I plunge into you. Deep and then shallow, quick and then slow, varying angles and pressure, I make you feel every inch in delicious detail as I explore your haven. You grip my arms, the table, my shirt, pulling me deeper, begging me to go harder, calling names I didn't think you knew. You curse me out then tell me you love me. You talk bad about my mother and then swear you want to be the mother to my kids. You scream "fuck you!" and then "fuck me!" You cum for me again and again and again.

Finally, you look at me with that deep, heavy, longing look as you groan:

"Daddy, I want you to cum for me."

I cannot reply because my breath has caught at your words. Your words are a signal to my loins and they are obeying on all cylinders. You raise up slightly and look deep into my eyes.

"Daddy, cum for me."

My breath and my pace quicken as I feel your love grip me in that sweet, tight, wet unquenchable liquid fire.

"Daddy," you whisper, as you spread your legs far and wide, offering, giving yourself to me totally and completely and without reservation. "Cum for me."

I give a muffled cry as my body begins to spasm. But before the first eruption, you push me away, slide down from the table, and slide me into your mouth. I damn near blackout from the sensation. Your hands grip my thighs as mine grip your hands, the table, your hair, fighting for balance, for breath, for sanity. Over and over my dick jumps between your lips as you drink me in. Your tongue swirls around the base, your hands cup and stroke my sac, your throat clenches around my quivering head. But more than that, it is the moans of pure satisfaction you make while you're doing it. The sound of real, sincere enjoyment. And when I see you slip your hand between your legs to play with yourself, I lose it and erupt again.

Finally, when I am spent, exhausted, finished, you lick your lips and then your finger and smile up at me.

"Was that lunch or dessert?" you ask me playfully.

"Shit, that was part of dinner." I fall back into a chair as you laugh and stand. I sit there, catching my breath as you move to retrieve our things. But when you bend over to pick up your shorts from the floor, I feel my dick begin to stiffen again. I lean forward and plant a kiss on your cheek.

"Oh," you say slyly. "I thought you were done."

I plant one on your other cheek.

"You better stop before you get yourself in trouble."

I plant a kiss on the lips between. You arch your back and sigh.

"Yes, you are officially in trouble."

"You had dessert," I say playfully, my lips beginning to start your love again, "now it's my turn..."

Canvas

The thick cloud of smoke poured toward the ceiling, coursing from his lips in grey curls and rivulets. He laid his head back against the couch, eyes closed, head nodding, mind, body, and soul at peace. The THC worked its way through his system but not as deeply as the mood, the music and the vibe. This was his favorite way to spend a day: jazz, ganja, and the proximity of a beautiful woman.

A pattering procession of skritches and scratches filled the small space. Short and insistent then slow and deliberate, they were a counterpoint harmony to the ticking of his nervous system. They were the sounds of art in creation.

"So what you think?" she asked him, brush poised over the waiting canvas. She was standing just the way he liked: hip cocked, arms loose but poised, almost as a bird anticipating flight, plump and luscious bottom lip caught lightly between her teeth as she frowned in concentration. He opened one eye and smiled.

"Question is: what do YOU think?"

"I think...you need to learn to answer a question." She turned and playfully flicked her brush at him. He laughed as the droplets of gold and scarlet spattered his clothes. Theirs was a familiar routine, and he'd long since learned to dress appropriately for her process.

"Aye, I'm just saying that beauty is in the eye of the beholder, but value is in the heart of the creator."

She humphed and curled her lip.

"You always think you deep when you high."

"Shit, I KNOW I'm deep -- and I GO deep." She laughed and he leaned forward and smacked her on the ass. She giggled, shooed him away, and turned back toward the canvas.

Her brush was a living thing. From it poured

visions and dreams and statements and referendums on reality. He was ever in awe of her ability to *see:* in, through and beyond life. Nothing seemed to escape her attention, nothing shirked her notice. She saw it all: saw it, stripped it bare, knew it to its core. But instead of turning away from it, mocking or reviling it, she took it, absorbed it, remade it and gave it life anew. Her eyes drew in life and birthed light. It was this, he thought, that drew him to her. That and a body that just would not quit.

At 5'9" she was "tall for a girl," a fact that intimidated many, but to him was a personal and preferred challenge. Tall himself, standing a shade over 6'3", he felt moved and motivated by a woman so lofty and lean. For she was long and sculpted, like a dancer or a model or some other grand calling given name and flesh. He teased her often, calling her his gazelle for the way the muscles formed shape and substance in her legs and flesh, fused with and fueled by a fire as pure as that from the sun. She was poetry in every motion — a poem made to be read on lips and fingertips.

He stood and moved silently behind her. Concentrating on her work, mind in that faraway place only she could view and inhabit, she didn't notice his approach – not until his arms circled her waist and his lips found her neck.

"What are you doing?" He could hear the edge of frustration in her voice. She hated to be interrupted, would fight if pushed too far. But he liked a woman with some fight in her: it made the rest better.

"Huh?" he said, nipping lightly at the soft chocolate skin on her collar bone.

"Don't 'huh' me," she said, swatting his hands that had drifted up to her breasts, "If you can 'huh' you can hear."

"Huh?" he said again, thumb grazing her nipple through the sports bra she wore. He felt it instantly stiffen and he smiled in anticipation.

"Boy, I done told you…" she began, but stopped and gasped as his other hand slid down the front of her tights and into the warm wet clutch of her love beneath. She arched back against him, an involuntary spasm of unanticipated ecstasy. He chuckled as he teased her, fingers sliding back and forth against her lips, dancing against the ever increasing moisture within.

"I'm sorry, ma'am; you were saying something?"

"I said…" The rest trailed off into a moan as his fingers entered her. Reaching back, she grabbed his head, holding him close as his lips and tongue played against her skin. From shoulder to collar to earlobe, he spared no inch or impulse. Her nerves fired in rapid and bright succession as he worked his machinations. She was a dish to be savored and he was a connoisseur.

Her hands found his as he pushed her bra up and over her breasts. As full and heavy as they were soft and warm, they were one of his favorite features. He could — and had — sat for what seemed like hours, slowly and methodically licking and sucking each one before eventually taking his attentions below. On those nights she'd lay back, wrapped in a cloud of incense and candles and sweet, slow jazz, and let him pay obeisance to her body.

Slowly he removed his hand from between her thighs. She looked back at him over her shoulder, eyes heavy-lidded and lips slightly parted, breath slow and husky. She bit her lip as she watched him lick his fingers clean, he smiling all the while. His loins stiffened as she turned and slid her tongue into his mouth, tasting herself on his lips. His hands encircled her back while hers his head, they both savoring the taste and feel and sheer nearness of each other.

Finally she pulled away and looked at him, one perfectly arched eyebrow raised in a question to which they'd both long decided the answer. With a smile in return, he took her hand and led her from the room.

They entered her bedroom, a sacred sanctum of a space. The furnishings were of the deepest shades, her dresser of mahogany, curtains of crimson, sheets and comforter the most midnight blue. It was a space that breathed silence and sensation and seduction.

As she moved around the room, lighting her many candles, he watched her. She was so fluid, so effortless in her movements and intentions, so confident in herself. Not for the first time he thanked the universe that he'd found her, someone so unique and yet to which he was so perfectly matched. If soulmates existed, he'd found his, and he planned never to let her go.

When the candles were all lit, she moved to another corner in which sat one of her favorite possessions and one of his earliest gifts: a vintage hi-fi turntable. Flipping through the stack of first-press vinyl records beside it, she smiled and pulled one from its sleeve. Settling the needle, she began to sway as the breathless static of the machine gave way to the soft sounds of Miles Davis' muted trumpet. As she danced, she pulled her bra up and off and slid her tights down her round hips. Clad now in nothing but waist beads and lust, she turned toward him.

He, too, was naked, having taken her cue, and stood before her, his manhood hanging low and heavy. Her eyes coursed over his skin, his creamy caramel complexion, sculpted arms and abs, his features so reminiscent of an African deity. She gazed lovingly and longingly at the thick black thatch of his pubic hair, and the mighty spear beneath. She sighed in anticipation as he pulled her close, his length pressing warm and heavy against her slick moistness.

He dropped his head and placed the softest kiss on her lips.

"You picked my favorite," he murmured, lightly licking and biting her flesh as she undulated against him.

"Don't I always?" she replied, sighing as his

lips found their way to the soft skin at her throat. She felt his breath quicken as her hands slid down between them and grabbed him, stroking and massaging with expert facility.

"How do you know me so well?" he asked, voice husky in her ear as he bit her earlobe and kissed the velvet skin beneath. She pushed back from him, taking his head in her hands and looking him directly in his eyes. He saw her seeing him, felt her searching him, was thrilled by the creation of a connection as pure and unshakeable as time itself.

"Because I know me. I'm you, and you're me, and that's how it was always meant to be."

"You tryna get poetic on me," he laughed, slapping her ass playfully.

"Hey, a bitch can be multifaceted," she said, cocking her head and patting her hair in mock-ratchetry.

"I know you're definitely multi- many things," he replied with a smile, and then dropped to his knees before her.

She moaned and twined her fingers in his hair as his lips found hers. With focused attention, he worked her slick portal, taking and savoring every drop she had to give. His tongue lapped the full length of her lips, long and slow, its warmth and roughness playing against each nerve in succession. He slid the tip between her lips, tasting the sweet, musky flesh therein, causing her legs to shiver in response. His large hands wrapped around her hips and cheeks, holding her steady as she rode out her love against his upturned face.

Parting her legs slightly, she tilted her hips forward, inviting him to more perfect access. He obliged. Sliding one hand up and between her thighs, he turned his lips to her clit, sucking it lightly as his fingers found and entered her. She shuddered at the sensation, his practiced digit softly probing her depths as his tongue lapped against her sensitivity. She groaned and ground against him, riding wave after wave of sensation as he brought her to and held her at the brink of ecstasy. Finally, when he knew she could stand it no longer, he increased speed and pressure, sucking and fucking her at the perfect pace, carrying her up and over the edge of a crashing orgasm. He held her hips as she bucked and shuddered against him, still licking and lapping, tasting and taking her through a series of shattering sensations.

Still wrapped in stuttering aftershocks, she found herself now wrapped in his arms as he stood and lifted her. Instinctively, her legs wrapped around his waist, gripping him tightly as her heart crashed in her chest. He held her close, near, allowing the calm and steady flow of his own pulse to soothe hers. She laid her head on his shoulder, arms locked around his broad back, hips undulating of their own rhythm and accord as they stood there, he caramel against her chocolate, their bodies so warm as to melt, blending perfectly against and into one another. And suddenly he was in her. With a practiced motion, she slid up and forward, catching him at the tip and sliding down onto him. They both moaned at the sudden thrilling sensation.

He slid his hands up under her legs and around to her ass, granting himself a better grip and she better purchase as she began to glide up and down his length. Slow and steady she moved against him, taking and bathing every inch. She sighed as he slipped and slid inside her, her body throbbing against his thrusts. She was so wet she dripped onto the floor beneath them, pearlescent pools of lust and satisfaction. She tilted her head back, eyes closed and lips parted as his teeth and tongue found her upturned nipples. Sucking and biting and licking, he set and controlled her rhythm as she rode out their ecstasy.

Finally, unable to stand any more, she slid off of him and down to the bed. His eyes met hers, confused — until she took him into her mouth. His head rocked back as he exhaled a deep sigh of pure satisfaction. Over and around him she licked, sparing no inch or surface or sensation. She lapped her cum from his shaft and where it had collected in droplets in the hair around the base. He moaned as her hands gripped and massaged him, her tongue suckling at his testes. And he groaned as she alternated in rhythm, one moment sucking his sac, the other forcing his head down her throat. Over and again, she sucked and suckled him, caressing and cajoling him to release. Finally, with a shuddering gasp, he did, muscles locked and vibrating as his dick pulsed inside her throat. Jet after jet of hot, thick cum coursed from his tip as he twitched against her tonsils. Her moans of satisfaction and desire extended and expanded the release. He felt that he might never stop, that he would cum forever, that this orgasm was his beginning, his end, his eternity.

Finally, spent, he pulled himself from between her lips, and collapsed on the bed beside her.

"Whoo," he laughed, voice fluttering as his

heartbeat fought its way back to normal. "You tryna drain a nigga?"

"Says the nigga tryna drink me dry," she responded, popping him playfully on the arm.

"Well, what can I say," he replied, eyes hooded with equal parts lust and mischief, "you're just so damn delicious." He turned toward her and reached for her hips, prepared to prove the truth of his words. She stopped him with a hand to his chest and a kiss to his lips.

"Just a minute, daddy," she whispered, and stood, crossing the room. From an ebony chest sitting atop her dresser she removed a large, soft-bristled paintbrush and several tins of pigment. These she had made herself from oils and herbs and other organics. Scarlet and gold and the green of grass and the blue of deep water at midnight and shade upon shade of life and light, all made by hand, all made my heart. She was a painter and life itself was become her canvas.

She turned back to him and watched him watch her as she crossed to him. In one smooth motion she straddled and took him inside of her. Rocking gently, acclimating them both to her warmth and rhythm, she opened one tin and dipped her brush. He lay his head back as he felt its bristles begin to glide against his chest. Down the deep cleft between his pectorals it went, down the line of his stomach, crossing the gulf of his navel, and continuing down to where the hairs above their sex met in one slick mesh. It was blue and smelled of lavender and honeysuckle and shea. Another tin opened and he smelled coconut and tea tree as she teased the tips of his nipples. Broad strokes opened his senses, filling him as he filled her. Another tin and this time it was sandalwood and cedar smoothing across his ribs and pelvis, delving deep into the center of his being and awareness. He felt elevated and uplifted, searching for and reaching a higher plane of existence and experience. Her brush etched not just his body but his being, painted not just his flesh but his fears and dreams and desires and ambitions and hopes and wantings and needs. She painted his soul across his skin and blended the perfect balance of life in their love and lust.

Not content to leave a canvas half-complete, she rose from him, sliding free from his shaft, slick and creamy with her love, turned, and settled her hips onto his face. As his lips found hers again, suckling at the sweet blush within, she took him into her mouth while taking her brush to his hips. Over and around his thighs she painted in crimson and purple and silver, adorning him with health, wealth, and nobility. She took her time with his toes as her tongue teased his tip. She rocked forward on her knees as she painted his, muffling his moans in her mound. She sighed as his thighs flexed under long strokes of sable and garnet. And she came as she covered his calves, bathing his flesh in hues of blues while bathing his face in a wash of her bliss. He kissed her cunt deeply and repeatedly and she felt a surge like the color of sunlight boil up and through her body.

Sated and satisfied, they lay together, skin and tints melding and flowing between them. Finally she rose and turned, coming to lay beside him, settling her head against his chest while his arms curled around her frame. He stroked her hair as she stroked his skin, playing along the lines and swirls she'd emblazoned on his body. She looked up to see him looking at her, his eyes deep as time and the love he felt for her. His lips curled into a sardonic smile as he spoke:

"So, what do you think?"

She laughed and answered, "Question is: what do YOU think?"

He laughed, and leaned forward to kiss her lips, her nose, her eyelids, her forehead.

"I think," he said into her crown, wrapping his arms around her as she slid atop him and settled into his embrace, "that beauty is in the eye of the beholder." And here he pulled back to look into her eyes, those eyes that saw him, searched him, made and molded him. He kissed her again.

"Yes, beauty is in the eye of the beholder, but value is in the heart of the creator. And baby," he sighed, tilting his hips and entering her again, "I love the way you create me."

Fín

Gotta Give a Lady what She Wants

He couldn't stand it.

He had to sit there next to her; hear her breathe; inhale her perfume, no doubt picked out with him in mind; feel the heat from her velvet skin; and succumb to each beat of her heart. Worst of all, he had to stare at those perfect lips, soft as a summer cloud, warm as a jungle rain, and sweet as his beloved peaches.

He couldn't stand it.

He shifted uncomfortably, trying to ease the ache in his loins, trying to shake the sudden maudlin poeticness that had settled over him, trying to pay attention to the professor, trying to forget the goddess that sat next to him. Out of the corner of his eye he saw her breasts heave with each breath, filling and stretching her shirt. The material was so tight and so thin that her nipples were outlined in perfect dark halos of temptation. Oh how he wanted them in his mouth, fighting his amorous tongue. (There was that poetry again.) Tearing his gaze away from her breasts, it fell instead into her lap, noticing how her full, soft thighs, seemed painted into her jeans. They seemed to laugh at him as she walked, taunting and teasing him, and he cursed himself for his weakness while simultaneously wishing he could hold them in his hands, caress her satin skin, kiss the inside of her thighs and work his way to his prize.

He couldn't stand it.

Worst of all, she was purposefully playing with him, glancing at him from the corner of her eye, breathing deeply, crossing and uncrossing her legs, toying with his hand as if she'd rather be toying with his dick. He tried to play it off, ask questions about the lesson, her thoughts on the subject, the weather, the price of tea in China (literally), something, anything to take his mind off of her and what she was doing to him. Finally, he couldn't take it anymore. The pressure and temptation were too much. He had to do *something*. So he reached over, took her chin in his hand, turned her head, and placed his lips upon hers in an insistent, deep, mind-numbing kiss. He couldn't believe he'd done it, figured at best he'd just shot to hell any chance he'd had with her, at worst signed up as a poster child of the #MeToo movement. But, instead, with a look that changed from amazement to lust in the blink of an eye, she leaned over and stuck her tongue in his mouth.

He was in heaven. At least that's what his dick told him. By now it was saying a whole helluva lot.

In whatever case, she was his now, he was hers, and he was at the pinnacle of fulfillment — that is until he felt her hand in his lap, caressing his dick through his jeans. He nearly lost it.

Once his eyes had finished rolling into the back of his head and regained focus, they resolved on her face. He started with a shock, because staring directly back at him were what he deemed the biggest, most beautiful, most lust-filled eyes he had ever seen. Those lips that he'd just tasted, those soft, perfect, cherubic lips, now curved in a way that said they were begging for a hell of a lot more than a kiss. He realized that he had died and gone to a very pleasant Hell.

Okay, this was what he'd been waiting for, dreaming of, planning for. This was his moment, and he was going to make the absolute most of it.

Taking her hand from his lap, he kissed her again, and quickly scanned the scene below them. They were in the very top row of a 300 seat auditorium. This being the last Friday before fall break, most of their fellow students had already cut out and head for home. He and she had stayed behind, however, two amongst a handful that were saving their coins to make the return trip during Christmas break. As such, they had the campus — and this class — virtually to themselves. Far below them, the professor droned on in a bored, desultory way, his mind on his own vacation mere hours away. Also below them were a smattering of students, spread out across the cavernous room. Everyone was lost in their own little worlds, too self-absorbed to know or care what was beginning to transpire in the shadows above them.

Smiling, he slid out of his seat and onto the worn, carpeted floor. He looked up at her as he undid her jeans, and she obligingly lifted herself so that he could slide them down. He groaned when he saw the peach pattern on her panties. This had to be a sign, he thought, not caring if it came from above or below. Leaning forward, he slid his tongue along her waistband, dancing it lightly across her softly heaving flesh. She moaned and he slowly pulled her panties down. What greeted him was a softly furred, neatly trimmed pussy that looked, smelled, and — yes, after giving it a lick — tasted like a peach. His dick doubled in size and pulsed so hard that his pants started jumping.

He slowly licked his finger and slid it into her, noting how warm and soft and tight she was. She sighed and squirmed, and he felt her muscles begin to squeeze around him. Tentatively, he licked his lips and then licked hers. He ran his tongue slowly up her slit, over and between the glistening lips, and then licked her engorged clit. He began to suck on it as his finger probed for her g-spot. She moaned and squeezed his head with her thighs.

"These are going to feel amazing around my waist," he thought as he ate. Licking and suckling and nuzzling, he consumed her like a full course Thanksgiving meal. His finger never stopped its work inside her, finally finding her g-spot, judging by her muffled screams. As he began to massage it, she went wild, bucking hard against the seat. Had there been more than 10 people in the room, including them, they might've gotten caught, but as it were, everyone else was still wholly and obliviously absorbed. He could care less. All that mattered to him was the fat, juicy pussy he was sucking on and the woman he knew he was falling in love with.

In mere moments, she reached climax. He could tell by the spasming of her cunt around his finger and her intensified, muffled screams. On instinct, he pulled his finger out and replaced it with his tongue, wrapping his lips around her mound. He didn't want to miss one drop of what she had to offer.

And she offered a lot.

She shook once and flooded his mouth with cum, wave upon wave of sweet nectar. The taste and sensation were extraordinary. He was in as much ecstasy as she and sucked on her clit fervently, hoping she would climax again. She did, surprising them both: she'd never before experienced a multiple. The second wave was less profuse but sweeter than the first, thick and creamy and delectable. He lapped it up greedily, cleaning her mound and the surrounding flesh with pure pleasure.

When he finally came up for air, he found her

staring at him, satiation and desire mingling in her eyes. She appeared spent but still in heat, lust radiating from her in waves like shimmers from rocks in the dessert. Grabbing him, she pulled him forward and granted him a deep, passionate kiss, their tongues dancing together in a language all their own.

Pulling away to catch his breath, he started to pull her pants back up, but she stopped him.

"I want to give you something," she said as she kicked off her shoes and stepped out of her jeans. She leaned forward, gave him another kiss, and started to unbutton his pants. He sighed and let her pull them down. His dick stood tall and rigid as an oak, the deep color of mahogany, pulsing like a live wire. Long and thick, it swayed softly and hungrily like a snake to a piping charmer. She leaned forward as if to kiss this deadly beast, but he stopped her.

"No," he said covering himself.

"But you..." she stammered.

"I know," he replied smiling, "but sometimes

it's better to give than to receive. And now," he said, pulling her into his lap and onto him, "I intend to give you all of this dick."

She moaned as she squirmed in his lap, adjusting herself to and around him. She began to move against him and he grabbed her waist to set their pace. Finding a rhythm, they rocked and bounced against each other. He palmed her ass and thighs as she rode him.

"How about doing me a favor," she moaned mid-stroke.

"What's that?" At this point he was willing to do and grant anything to keep this moment from ending.

"How about sucking on these?" And she pulled up her shirt to reveal her breasts. They were as soft and full as he'd imagined, the nipples hard and dark and jutting proudly into the air. He bit his lip as he stared at them.

"Well, I mean, since you asked so nicely," he

murmured, and leaned forward to take them into his mouth. He took one hand from its place on her soft, round ass, and moved it, instead, to one of her soft, round breasts. Kneading it softly, he moved his lips and attention to the other, suckling it like a hungry baby.

"Ooo, yes, daddy. Just like that." She moaned, arching her back and pulling him further into her. The sensation set her to riding with renewed fervor. Recognizing the signs of her impending climax, he alternated between her breasts, sucking the hard buds of her nipples, kissing the soft flesh on their undersides, nipping at the skin between, and licking along the crease beneath. All the while he maintained the pace and rhythm of his stroke.

Suddenly he felt her legs and cunt clench around him. She was coming for a third time, shaking and spasming in his lap. The erotic strain seemed to get the best of her and she fell against him, squeezing his head, pawing at his back and gripping his ears.

"Ouch, that hurts," he laughed, trying to free himself from her grip.

"Sorry," she gasped. "I just...got...caught up." Leaning back, she fanned herself, catching her breath and regaining her composure. She looked at him beneath her, he admiring her body, running his hands along her skin, enjoying the sight and feel of her. She felt his dick, hard and thick, humming as it nestled deep within her flesh. She smiled a wicked little smile.

Leaning forward and grabbing the back of his seat for better position and traction, she bent down and bit his lip.

"I don't like you judging me," she said, licking his lips as she began to undulate atop him.

"I wasn't..." he started, but she stopped him with another kiss.

"Like I said, I don't like you judging me. So let's see how you react when you cum." And with that, she took off with a fury, bouncing and jouncing on his dick like a runaway horse.

"Sweet shit," he said around a nipple, hanging on for dear life. She fucked him with a ferocity that left him breathless. She was as passionate as she was relentless, taking him fast and hard, long and deep. She fucked him like she was trying to lay claim to him, to his soul, etching his name across the inside of her womb. She was fucking him into ownership, and he was more than ready to hand over the deed.

"Baby," he groaned, breath catching in his throat as it fought its way past the racing of his heart. "Slow down! I can't..."

"No." She silenced him with another kiss. "I want to feel you cum inside of me. I want to feel every...last...drop." She punctuated her words with a series of thrusts that pushed him up and to the edge. With a renewed energy and sense of purpose, he found and met her rhythm.

"Well," he mumbled, gasping with the effort of holding back, "mama always told me that you gotta give a lady what she wants." And with that, he let loose.

He fucked her with all the passion he could muster, sucking her nipples and pawing her ass. She kissed his lips, his neck, bit his ears, sucked his tongue. They were a ravaged beast of ecstasy and excess, fucking their way to the brink of an epic explosion. And then it happened. His dick twitched and seemed to grow double. His balls pulled up against his body. He felt his orgasm hammering at the base of his shaft, the base of his spine, the base of his very soul. This was it, the moment of pure and perfect release into the object of his pure and perfect passion.

His trembling shaft must have quivered just right, because when the first shot came boiling up and out of him, steaming through his dick, shooting like a geyser inside of her, her walls spasmed and she climaxed again. They came together, the feeling growing and intensifying until they both screamed, she into the top of his head, he into the soft flesh between her breasts. Someone near the front seemed to hear and looked up and back, but could only see a single, tall body, they being unified so perfectly.

She slumped over him, savoring the aftershocks, and moaned into his ear.

"Damn, that was good. I wish we would've done it sooner."

"Yeah, me too," he confessed, "but sometimes you gotta let things progress naturally."

"I'm with that." She paused and then continued with a smile: "How bout we let things naturally progress again tomorrow?"

"Sure," he replied slyly as she slid off of him and they began to fix their clothes, "if you think you can handle it."

"Don't get too big a head, now," she said, punching him playfully in the arm and laughing.

"Well, my head is big enough." Her eyes followed where he pointed and she found herself staring, amazed to see it standing proudly, glistening with their combined love, vibrating still with heat yet to be released.

"Well, well, well," she murmured, lowering her head. "It *is* plenty big." And she wrapped her lips around it, sucking him in slowly.

He sat back and sighed, watching and listening to her work.

Did he stop her this time?

No.

Because after all, you gotta give a lady what she wants.

Happy Endings

"Okay, Mrs. Davis," Tariq said, escorting the woman to and through the sliding bamboo door. "We'll stop by the desk on your way out and Tessa will get you set up for your next appointment."

The woman stopped, turned, and stood on her tiptoes to give him a hug. The women in the reception area craned to watch, amusement and envy mingling in the looks on their faces.

"Thanks, T. You are a certified lifesaver," Mrs. Davis gushed, near blushing. She saw the other women's looks and knew what they were thinking. As if reassuring both them and herself, she twisted the large wedding ring on her finger.

Tariq laughed, his voice deep and melodious. The ladies in the room fought a collective groan of desire. His voice seemed to fall like a warm rain, settling like silk into each woman's ears — and places

58

a few steps lower.

"I don't know about saving lives, but I do what I can."

"Yes," she replied, eyes averted, a shy smile on her lips. "You sure do."

Accompanying her to the desk, he waited while the receptionist penciled her in and then handed her her appointment card. Tariq elected not to notice the eyes following him across the room as he escorted her through the seating area and to the spa door. He placed his large, finely boned hand on the small of her back as he opened the door for her.

"See you next week?" He smiled, his eyes twinkling with warmth and life.

"I wouldn't miss it for the world," she replied, returning his smile. As she stepped out and onto the sidewalk, the women inside couldn't help but notice a certain extra sway to her step. They all fully understood why.

Tariq was an absolute specimen, the very

picture of black male exceptionalism. Tall at six-foot-five, he was long and lithe, muscles finely and perfectly chiseled across the breadth and depth of his frame. His shoulders were broad and immaculately defined, tapering down to a narrow waist and solid hips. His arms, bare to the shoulder in a sleeveless linen tunic, were gorgeously sculpted, the muscles taut as steel cables under his burnished skin. They ended in hands that seemed large and strong enough to break pure granite, but that they knew were gentle enough to handle the most delicate flower. Pecan brown with long, thick, flowing dreadlocks, he looked like some West Indian deity, come down from on high to visit them.

Turning back into the room, Tariq stepped to the receptionist's desk. Perusing the appointment book, he smiled as he noticed and called the next name.

"Chanelle. Back so soon?"

The woman in question stood. Five foot six,

lean yet curvy, a runner's build. Strong calves curved upward into thick, well-muscled thighs, both crowned by a perfectly round and buoyant behind. This switched perceptibly as she walked toward Tariq. She placed her hand on his arm and smiled, a mischievous twist to her lips.

"What can I say? I've got some kinks that need to be worked out and you're the best man I know for the job."

The women in the room stifled their reactions. Some rolled their eyes at her forwardness. Others cut their eyes in jealousy. Near all, however, tried to hide the desire radiating like heat from beneath their lids. Tariq, for his part, laughed again, a deep yet free chuckle. He was used to these reactions and had become inured to them. It was all part of the mystique.

"Well," he said stepping aside to let her pass him as he escorted her to the room, "let's see what we can do about that."

The women in the waiting area craned again to watch them go, eyes and minds already painting images in their imaginations. The receptionist, Tessa, looked up from her desk and bit back a laugh. She was accustomed to this, but still found it amusing. Smiling, the laughter still playing around her eyes, she inquired politely:

"Would any of you ladies care for a bottle of water? We wouldn't want you getting too thirsty..."

***

Tariq ushered Chanelle into the room and quietly closed the door. He took her purse from her and set it on a nearby table on which, also, lay his phone, which he now tapped, cueing up a playlist he knew she liked. The soft strains of Musiq Soulchild began to fill the room alongside the warm scents of sandalwood and cedar emanating from his oils and many candles. She kicked off her shoes and stepped toward the screen behind which she would undress.

Her voice came to him from beyond the partition.

"So how've you been?"

Tariq chuckled.

"Since last time?"

"You say it like it was yesterday or something." There was a slight hint of abused yet amused reproach in her voice.

"Not quite. Just the day before." They both laughed as she stepped from behind the screen, clad in a short silk robe. She flicked his arm as she made her way to the table.

"Can I help it that my muscles choose to tense up on short notice?"

"I don't know," he replied, setting towels for her head and hips on the table, and pulling his cart to his side. "Can you?"

"I cannot," she responded loftily, and, with a flourish, removed the robe, revealing her smooth, naked body underneath.

Tariq raised an eyebrow in appreciation. He'd

63

seen her nude several times before, but he never tired of the sight. Above her wide, full hips, her waist narrowed almost impossibly into a stomach devoid of an ounce of fat. Above, her breasts sat soft and full, firm C cups, high and perky. Below, her thighs framed a thick thatch of dark brown hair, neatly trimmed at the edges, but full and lush between. Behind it, the lips of her sex were just visible, thick and pouty and delectable.

As she turned to lie down, Tariq noticed, not for the first time, how her perfectly smooth caramel skin seemed to glow like brass in the light of the candles suffusing the room. Her flesh embraced and absorbed the flames, then returned them, radiating its own sweet, slow fire.

Crossing her arms beneath her head, Chanelle sighed as she settled into the warm, worn leather of the table. Tariq placed a soft terry towel over her hips and smoothed errant hairs from the nape of her neck. She inhaled, the heady scents of lavender and jasmine working deep into her lungs as he un-stopperd and poured the oils into his hands and then onto her skin.

"So what's been new?" Chanelle asked, voice low and dreamy as she began to relax under his fingertips. Tariq laughed again, the sound trilling across her eardrums and spine.

"I don't know that there's been enough time for there to be anything 'new.'"

"Well, what's old, then? Talk to me. Tell me something. You know how I hate just laying here in silence."

Tariq smiled as he gathered another handful of oil and began to work it into her shoulders.

"I don't know that there's really anything 'old,' either. Tell you what: let's make this easier. Tell me what you've got going on with you."

"Oh," Chanelle replied, feigning diffidence. "If you really want to know..."

Tariq laughed as she began. This was their routine. She'd begin by asking about his day before launching into a recounting of her own. He didn't mind, though. He liked to listen to her talk. She was interesting. Her life wasn't full of the petty inanity that he often found in many women. She had no time for the endless squabbles and betrayals and bitterness that colored a lot of other women's conversations; she was far too focused on her future for that kind of foolishness. Her conversation, instead, concerned her dreams and ambitions, and she spoke of them not in the nebulous, vague way that some did, but in the matter of fact tones of a person actively pursuing and accomplishing them. She spoke of contracts negotiated, leases signed, monies procured and invested. She spoke of the life she was building for herself to live, and he found it infinitely intriguing and inspiring.

Tariq was standing in front of her, working the tight muscles at the base of her neck when he heard her laugh softly.

"Yes?" he inquired his voice wafting down

from above.

"I can see him." For emphasis, she poked him with a finger, causing him to roll his eyes in mock annoyance.

"Will you stop that?"

"Why? You the one that did it," she said, poking him again. He swatted her hand away.

"I did not."

"Who did, then?" she asked, poking him with both hands this time. He laughed, rolled his eyes again, and let her amuse herself.

"Put that on God, not me."

"Oh, so is that who I have to blame — or thank — for this?"

He looked down and saw a smirk and devilish twinkle in her eye. He sighed and shook his head, his face taking on the long-suffering mien of a martyr.

"Must you always?" he asked, resuming the massage.

"You know I do," she replied, now openly

rubbing him. "It's not my fault he's always looking at me."

"Is that right?"

"It is." She grabbed and stroked him for emphasis. "Just always looking at me."

To be fair, she was essentially right. Hanging long and heavy, Tariq's massive penis could be seen as a solid shadow beneath the light linen. It seemed to move and sway with a life and rhythm all its own, like a desert cobra waiting to be charmed from its home. Chanelle licked her lips at the thought of how charmingly deadly it really was.

As Tariq's hands worked their way down Chanelle's back, Chanelle worked loose the knot in the drawstring of his pants. As his fingers reached the swell of her hips, he felt the gentle pull of her lips as she took the tip of his penis into her mouth. They sighed simultaneously.

"Mmm," she moaned, tongue twirling around him, mouth getting wetter and warmer by the moment. "Just as tasty as I remember." Tariq chuckled, leaning forward slightly to gain better access to both her back and her throat.

"You thought that it might have changed in two days?"

"You never know. Somebody might have come along and taken it while I was away."

Tariq leaned back and cupped her chin, raising her eyes to him. They were a soft and natural hazel that almost glowed in the candlelight. His own were gray, gray as soft summer clouds full of sweet rain. His eyes always made her wetter, and hers made him burn hotter.

"You know it's not like that," he said, smiling down at her. "I'm not that kind of guy." She smiled back at him, pulling her lips away from his dick with a slight slurp. She kissed the tip, licking their combined moisture.

"I should hope not. I'd hate to have to cut a bitch up in here." They laughed at the thought and

69

the image and the fact that she was completely serious. She was sophisticated but that didn't mean she was soft.

Tariq reached down and slapped her playfully on the ass.

"I'd hate that, too," Tariq smiled, gliding his hands along the warm, pliable flesh of her upturned cheeks. She sighed and rolled her hips at the pressure of his touch. She could feel and he could smell her get wet in response and anticipation. The temperature seemed to rise in the room. "I don't know if I could lose my best customer to jail."

"Hey, you know a chick keeps bail money and a lawyer on retainer. I do NOT play 'bout mine's." Tariq laughed as she flipped her hair and smacked on an imaginary wad of gum. Chanelle was definitely a handful, possibly several hands full, but he liked her that way. Bold, brash, confident, sure of herself and her place in the world. She was, as the saying goes, what every woman wanted to be and every man wanted to be with. It was an intoxicating combination.

Tariq chuckled, pouring himself another handful of oil which he slowly worked through his fingers before placing them back on her back. Chanelle sighed and stretched lazily before taking hold of the shaft of his dick, still swinging heavily above her, and sliding it back into her mouth. She hummed in satisfaction, the vibrations rippling through his glans where it rested against her tonsils. His eyes lowered as the sensations coursed through him.

"No," he said, half to her and half to himself, "you most definitely do not play."

Tariq's hands worked along her body as her mouth worked along his dick. His fingertips found the softest spots of her flesh while her tongue tasted his hardest. He kneaded and plied her with thumbs and palms while she stroked and suckled him with lips and throat. It was a symphony of sensation — and it was only getting warmed up.

Leaning forward, Tariq placed his hands under

71

her hips, tilting them up and toward him. She obligingly spread her knees, anticipating what was coming next. Arching over her, Tariq placed a kiss on the center of her spine before traveling downward, his full, soft lips, alternating with his broad, warm tongue as it trailed along her skin. Reaching her hips, he placed a kiss on the dimples there, then on each of her upturned cheeks. Finally, with one smooth, sensuous motion, he licked down the crack of her ass and into the deep well of her warm, wet pussy. She arched her back and moaned around his rod as he began to eat her from above.

Her hands gripped and worked the strong muscles in his thighs as he slowly fucked her throat. For her part, she spread and undulated beneath him, offering herself ever more fully to his probing lips and tongue. She could feel the tips of his dreads swaying like the fringes of a silk curtain, swishing against her skin. The sensation was electric, sending shockwaves through her synapses in rushes of lust and ecstasy.

After several minutes of blissful indulgence, he extricated himself from the sweet torture of her lips. Flipping her over and around, he pulled her to him, her thighs coming to rest against his own. Smiling down into her eyes, he raised her legs and then slid himself into her in a single, thick stroke, the combination of their oral ministrations, mixed with the warm oils with which their skin glistened, making his entry smooth and seamless. She arched her back and moaned as he penetrated her to the hilt.

Smiling to himself, he traced one finger down the line that ran from her throat to her navel.

"So what'll it be today, Ms. Chanelle?" She trembled as his hands rifled her bush, finding and tweaking the hard bud beneath.

"You already know, daddy," she responded, her eyes closed, lips slightly parted, her breath coming in soft pants of expectation.

Tariq set himself a sedate pace, gliding in and out of her slick, warm wetness. Stroking her womb, he resumed stroking her flesh, his hands working in rhythm and tandem. Pushing her legs forward, he took one foot and then the other, thumbs easing the tension in their tendons. He plied the soft heels and arches, placing kisses on the latter as he applied oil to her insteps. He massaged and then sucked each toe in succession, drawing gasps of pleasure accompanied by tiny tremors he could feel deep inside her.

More oil, and now over her ankles to her calves. Firm and round, they flexed with each stroke of his sex and relaxed under the strokes of his hands. Stretching and smoothing them, he worked them over until they glistened like amber in the candlelight.

He spread her thighs, then, and paused, taking in the sight before him: the fat, firm lips of her sex wrapped around the fat, firm length of his. Her bush, soft and curly, glistened with the combined sheen of sex and oil, droplets caught on the tips of the hairs like raindrops after an August rain. Her clit gleamed rosy and wet, hard and proud, as it pulsed in time with the beat of the dick lodged beneath it.

Licking his lips at the remembrance of licking hers, he ran his fingertips up the inside of her thighs, making her tremble.

"I can tell you went to the gym this morning." His voice rose from his chest as if from a well. It came out deep and husky, laced with his thrumming desire. She purred when she heard it, the resonance achieving a frequency that made it seem like he was speaking directly to and through her vagina.

"You know me entirely too well," she responded, stretching herself before and beneath him, flexing like a feline in heat, and allowing him to admire the fruits of her dedication — and other things. He laughed as he suddenly pushed himself into her even deeper, pulling a startled, ecstatic gasp from her lips.

"One could say that, yes."

She opened her eyes to see the amusement in his, then reached up and slapped him playfully on the chest.

"Curb the jokes, sir," she said and then sighed as he resumed motion inside her.

"Yes ma'am," he replied, a smile still hovering on his lips.

His hands worked the soft flesh of her inner thighs, kneading the taut muscles as they flexed against his thrusts. Placing her legs together, he pushed them both up and back, giving himself access to her outer thighs as well as deeper points between. As his hands gripped, worked, and massaged her skin, the walls of her womb gripped, worked, and massaged his shaft.

Lowering her legs, he wrapped them around his waist and pulled her closer. She moaned as he assumed a new angle and position inside of her. His hands began to work the tight expanse of her abdominals, fingers dancing along its curves and valleys as it trembled beneath his touch. He pressed one heavy palm into the space beneath her belly button and felt himself sliding in and out of her.

76

Pressing down harder, he was rewarded with feeling her shudder as his shaft grazed her g-spot. He chuckled as he fucked her.

"What's got...you...so amused, sir?" she asked, voice catching at the mounting sensations.

"I was just thinking that I should charge you double, seeing as how you're getting two massages in one."

"Oh, is that what this is?" she laughed, tightening the grip of her legs around his hips, pulling him closer and deeper.

"Yup," he replied, smiling. "Not everybody gets to experience being massaged from the inside and outside simultaneously."

"They'd better not," she said with playful vehemence. "But hey, that's why I tip so good."

"Is that right?"

"Yes, sir. Good tips for good service."

"Oh," he said, tracing the skin along her ribcage, feeling the push and pull of her breath as her chest rose and fell with his thrusts. "It's just 'good,' is it?"

She grabbed his hands and slid them up to her breasts. He took them, reveling in their fullness and weight, then gripped them forcefully, just how he knew she liked it. She moaned and pulled him closer, her hands squeezing his upon her while her hips worked circles against him.

"Oh, no, baby. It's better than good; it's great."

He smiled indulgently for this was obvious; they'd left "good" behind a long time ago.

Smile still on his lips, he leaned down and wrapped them around one taut nipple. She gasped as his tongue flicked roughly across its surface, his lips circling and teasing. She moaned and panted as he moved to the other and then back, giving them equal, amorous attention. Finally, she had to bite back a scream when she felt him bite her, his strong, white teeth holding her in the perfect, excruciating balance

78

between pain and pleasure. Her eyes flickered open, finding and then staring into his. Her voice, when she spoke, was thick and heavy as honey.

"Baby, I'm ready."

He pulled away and from within her. She sat up to meet him, her whole body radiating lusty anticipation. Gathering another handful of oil, he poured some into her hands before working the rest into his fingers. Slowly, eyes locked on hers, he slipped two fingers up and into her as her hands wrapped around his dick. With his free arm he pulled her close, kissing her as they began to stroke each other toward orgasm.

His thick fingers filled her nearly as much as his dick had. She thrilled at their warmth and strength, so forceful yet so gentle. He knew and worked her most sensitive spots, playing her womb like a finely tuned instrument. His thumb massaged her clit in strong, fluid circles that sent her head spinning in ecstasy. She moaned into his mouth as their tongues tangled in a dance of liquid lust.

Her hands upon him were as warm, smooth, and tight as her walls had been. His nerves sparked and sparkled as she stroked his shaft, a million tiny fireworks setting his soul ablaze. She applied perfect pressure and pace, pulling and tugging and gripping and gliding, driving him toward climax. His breath matched hers in pants and quavers, their lips and tongues tossing and twining together.

As one, in a single, glorious moment, they trembled and came, she squirting her pleasure against his groin and thighs as he released against her stomach and breasts. Their climax lasted several seconds, neither wanting to release the other, pushing themselves to higher, more perfect heights. On and on it went, each filling and fulfilling a harmony as perfect and poignant as time itself.

Finally, spent, they separated. Their love mixed and sparkled with the oil upon their skin, painting them in hues of sandalwood, cinnamon, and sex.

She ran her fingers across her chest, gathering the creamy coils of his lust, licking them off of her fingers and hands with uninhibited pleasure. He responded, pulling his fingers from the warm clutch of her sex and placing them between his lips, taking and savoring every drop. They kissed, then, tasting each other on their lips and tongues.

"Mmm," she murmured, her tongue still gliding along his, "that's pretty good."

"About as good as it was two days ago," he replied, laughing, and then dodged as she swung at him.

"Gah! So a chick needs her regular fix. Sue me."

In response, he gathered her into his arms. She felt their strength, like steel wrapped in the softest silk; felt his warm skin, the color of caramel that had been baptized in sunlight; felt his sex, long, heavy, and hot between them. And, finally, she felt his heartbeat, strong and steady and pulsing in perfect unison with her own.

"I'd much rather just make love to you," he said, pressing his lips to her forehead, her eyelids, her throat, her lips, so soft, full and yielding.

"Aww," she pouted.

"Aww?" he asked, eyebrow raised in genuine confusion.

She reached down and grabbed him then, a mischievous twinkle in her eye. She stroked him until he stood proud and strong once more.

"I thought you might just wanna fuck me." She smiled and he saw in her eyes life and light and love and lust and more than a little bit of challenge. He laughed as he turned her around and bent her over the table, she giggling while wiggling her hips, waiting for him. She drew a sharp breath as pleasure rushed through her spine along the length of his shaft, entering and filling her depths.

"I mean, if you insist. And hey," he said, glancing over at the clock on the wall, "my next session doesn't start for another thirty minutes. Let's see what we can do about that tip..."

Higher

"Ladies and gentlemen, we have reached cruising altitude and the captain has turned off the fasten seatbelt sign. You are now free to move about the cabin."

"Like hell I will."

"Baby, it's perfectly safe."

"Like hell it is."

Denise bit back a laugh. Deandre was a pitiful sight. His hands were locked in a death grip on the small armrests, his fingers damn near leaving indentations in the plastic. Beads of perspiration dotted his brow as he stared into the middle distance, seemingly trying his level best to ignore where he was and what he was doing.

The trip had been planned for months and still had been almost grounded. Why? Because Deandre was terrified of leaving the ground. "If man was meant to fly, God would've given him wings," was his constant refrain. Denise tried everything she could think of to reassure him. She invited friends over who were stewards and stewardesses; had her father, a veteran Air Force pilot, call and give him a pep talk; recounted her thousands of hours spent in the air, traveling across the country and the globe. Nothing worked. She even tried the old "you're statistically safer in a plane than a car" routine. His response: "One, cars don't sit 300 people at a time, which skews the numbers considerably. Two, cars don't travel at 500 miles an hour. And three, and most importantly, cars don't plummet 30,000 feet at 32 feet per second squared. So, no: I am NOT safer in a plane." Finally, it had come down to the promise of prescription drugs and as many glasses of free liquor as they could manage that got him onboard.

They were on their way to Atlanta for a book signing, Deandre just having released a barnstorming first novel. It had literally blazed up the bestseller lists, topping critic and consumer reviews in every category. Everyone from hip-hop movers and shakers to the biggest social media influencers were on it, and Oprah had given it her coveted golden stamp of approval. The book was burning through stores and Dre's company had booked him for a whirlwind, 30 city, signing and press tour. As his manager, marketing consultant, and number one muse, Denise was running the tour with him. And it was a rocky road to run.

"Baby, it's okay to breathe," Denise reassured her husband for literally the 15th time. "Remember: Inhale. Exhale. Inhale. Exhale."

"I'm *in* Hell," he retorted, but doing the breathing exercises nonetheless. The veins on his forehead and arms that had been standing out in sharp relief ever since they boarded and took their seats seemed to finally be receding. Denise took this as a relatively positive sign.

"There you go, baby. You're doing great. See,

we're good. Ten minutes in and only 3 and a half more hours to go."

Dre shot her a look of such sheer panic that Denise instantly regretted her comment. She stroked his arm to calm him as he started to hyperventilate.

"Baby! Baby, calm down!" she said, soothing him. Inside, she had to admit that she was laughing, his terror almost comical in its extremeness. But she knew better than to do it openly. Deandre was a big man, 6'3" and near 300lbs of solid, chocolate muscle, and though he was generally a gentle giant, she did NOT want to find out how that giant would react in an enclosed space when pushed into a panic. She had a sudden image of the Hulk Helicarrier rampage in the Avengers movie, and shuddered.

"Just calm down, baby. It's gonna be okay. Everything is fine. Just forget I said anything."

"That'd be easier to do if you'd stop saying things," he ground out between gritted teeth. Those veins, once sinking toward dormancy, had come back with a vengeance. Denise shook her head and popped him on the arm, chiding him as if he were a child — and trying to keep from telling him that he was acting like one.

"Now, don't be mean. I was just trying to help."

"Yeah, well, how about you help me to another one of those pills. And where's that drink cart? Shouldn't there have been a drink cart by now?"

"Baby, you know what the doctor said: you can only take a maximum of 2 pills every 6 hours, and you took those right before we boarded, so you're not due for another dose until well after we land. Also, the drink cart will be along but it will probably be a few minutes as the stewardesses have just been allowed to get up and move around and therefore have to get everything ready. It's coming, though, baby, I promise."

"Make it come faster, please, or they might not make it in time."

"In time for what?"

"The massive coronary I'm about to have."

She did laugh then, a light, airy, musical laugh. It was a sound he loved, one of the things that had initially attracted him to her, though at this precise moment, "attraction" was the farthest thing from his mind.

"Woman..." he began, using a tone that she knew too well. It was his "I'm getting serious" voice, and she knew that when Dre got serious, he meant it. He was a good natured guy — kind, thoughtful, openhanded with everyone, quick to smile, laugh, and joke — but he was still all man, and when the man voice came out, it was serious business. She quickly patted his arm again to soothe him.

"I'm sorry, baby," she said, caressing his chest, smoothing the wrinkles of his shirt and the frayed edges of his nerves. "I didn't mean to laugh. I know this is tough for you and I know it's scary. But I also need YOU to know something."

"What's that?" he asked, turning and eyeing her suspiciously. She leaned in and kissed him, her lips full, soft and warm against his. She leaned back and looked him in his eyes.

"I'm right here with you, the whole way through. I'm not going anywhere, okay?" She took his hand and recited their favorite vow. "From birth to earth."

"From womb to tomb," he continued. Then, "For ever..."

"...and for always."

He smiled, then, the first time in what seemed like forever, and Denise smiled back at him, falling in love all over again with this strong, beautiful, handsome man.

Dre settled back into his seat, the plush, warm leather cradling his massive frame. He shifted and scooted, working to find the most comfortable position for the journey ahead. Eyes closed, something approximating peace — mixed with a heavy dose of resignation — adorning his face, he sighed and took Denise's hand.

"For ever and for always, babe. You and me together. You right here by my side."

"Exactly," she responded before loosening her grip. "Right after this." She stood up and his eyes immediately snapped open in panic.

"Where are you going?!" he near shouted, clutching for her hand.

"To the bathroom. Baby, I've been needing to pee since we got to the airport, and if I don't go now, well, I'm still gonna go now, but it'll be here, not there."

"But baby..." he whined, eyes brimming with renewed and mounting fear.

"No 'buts,' baby, I gotta go. And it'll only be a minute, I promise."

Dre surprised her, then, by untying (he'd said "Screw buckling; I don't trust their maintenance like that") his seatbelt and joining her in the aisle. Her shock was evident on her face.

"Baby..." she began, but he stopped her.

"Hey, where *you* go, *I* go. We said 'together,' and gaht dangit, we gone *do* together."

Denise shook her head and laughed as she took his hand and led him back to the lavatory.

The stewardesses smiled at them as they passed through the galley. Veterans of the game, they knew how jumpy the extremely anti-airplane could be, so sympathized with both the individuals and their travel companions. And actually, Dre was far from the worst that this particular crew had seen. For instance, there was the one passenger that suddenly developed an acute onset of extreme claustrophobia and tried to open the emergency exit door mid-flight. THAT was an exciting day. Compared to the threat of explosive decompression at 35,000 feet, Dre was an absolute cakewalk.

"Do we know what we'd like to drink today?" one stewardess asked them, smiling. "And how many?" she added, with a wink to Denise. Denise laughed in reply.

"A white wine for me, three Crown and cokes for the big baby, here."

"I am *not* a baby," Deandre mumbled as both ladies laughed.

"Don't worry, sir, I fully understand. We just serve drinks; we don't judge."

Dre muttered a quick thanks as Denise laughed and led him into the bathroom.

This being first class, the stall was larger and roomier than those in the lower cabins. Still not big, by any means, it managed to hold them both relatively comfortably. Dre flipped the "Occupied" switch, and leaned back against the door as Denise dropped her pants and hit the seat with a contented, grateful sigh.

"Thank you, Jesus," she exhaled.

"I bet you feel five pounds lighter," Dre chuckled from his vantage.

"Nobody should come in here for 35, 45

93

minutes," she completed the line, and they laughed together. Done, she wiped and stood and turned to the sink. Looking at him in the mirror, she nodded toward the commode.

"Do you want to go ahead and go? I know you're not trying to get back up again."

"You right. The less I move around in this airborne aluminum can, the better."

He stepped around her and to the toilet, then unzipped and pulled himself out. Big, dark, and thick like the rest of him, his dick hung there, heavy in his hand. Watching him in the mirror, she licked her lips as she eyed it, one eyebrow cocked appraisingly.

"Well, well, well, Mr. Williams; what big dong you have there."

Dre rolled his eyes at her.

"Really, D? Really?"

"What?" she said innocently. "Can I help it that you've got a literary dick?"

Dre rolled his eyes again. Denise stood in the

mirror, watching as he finished relieving himself, dabbed, and then prepared to put it away. She stopped him, reaching out and taking hold of it.

"Seriously, Mr. Williamson, how do you manage that thing? Call Ahab; I've found the Great Black Whale!"

Dre shuffled around her and to the sink, dick still out and in her hand. He shook his head at her.

"Denise, love: you need help."

"Help?" She stood, fondling him with one hand, tapping her lip with the other. " 'Help.' I know I've got one for this one... Ooh, ooh!" she said, actually bouncing with excitement. "You is big, you is thick, you is super potent!"

Dre laughed despite himself, his penis jouncing in her palm. Denise was crazy, but she was *his* crazy, and that's really the best crazy to have. He leaned over to kiss her.

"You," *kiss* "need" *kiss* "help."

She kissed him back and smiled against his

lips.

"You might be right, but at least I got you feeling better." He smiled, acknowledging that this was true. He started to put himself away again, but, again, she stopped him.

"And you know what would *really* make you feel better?" She dropped to her knees in front of him. Shocked and discombobulated, he fought to stop her, trying, vainly, to wrangle her hands from the gorilla grip they'd assumed on his dick. She evaded his attempts, dodging and slapping his flailing hands away, finally forcing him to quit in frustration.

"Denise!" His voice edged with consternation and a tinge of panic, but this time for a completely non-flight related reason. "We can't do that in here!"

"And why not?" she replied, hands already working up and down his shaft.

"Because...because..." He was finding it hard to concentrate as she worked him over. She was phenomenally good at that, knowing all the twists and touches that made him twitch. "Because," he tried again, and then finished triumphantly, "what if someone has to use the bathroom!" He was rather proud of himself for having come up with that bit of logic in an, admittedly, tight spot. This time, it was Denise's turn to roll her eyes. She spoke as she stroked.

"Baby, we're in first class which means, one, that there's more than one bathroom, so people can just use the other one. Also, you probably didn't notice, what with your eyes squinched shut from the moment we got to the airport, but this flight is really light, especially up here. There's probably 75 people spread out over this entire plane, and only 5 of us in first class. Ergo, we are highly unlikely to be disturbed."

Dre had to admit that that was a good point. To be fair, though, he wasn't in the right frame of mind to give it much scrutiny, his brain having surrendered some of its processing power to his dick, now hard and pulsing in her hands. The way that she was now also fondling his balls as she stroked didn't help matters either. Mustering what remaining cognition he possessed, he tried again.

"Okay, maybe not the passengers, but what about the stewardesses? They use these bathrooms, right?"

"Yes, they would," Denise conceded, "IF it wasn't a part of their training to take care of such things before and after flights. Except in extreme emergencies," she felt him tense up and increased her hand speed. "NOT that kind. The bathroom version." She felt him relax and resumed. "As I was saying, except in cases of extreme emergency, they don't go mid-flight. Besides," she said, now stroking that area behind the head, the one that always made his knees get soft and shaky. "Me and ol girl have already worked it out."

Dre looked down at her, confused.

"What do you mean?" he said, trying to

assimilate and process this information against the sensations rippling through his shaft and up his spine. Denise continued her ministrations as she explained.

"You remember that little conversation we had before coming in here?"

"Yeah." It took a second, but then Dre's face lit up with the dawn of understanding. "You mean...she knew?" Denise laughed that musical laugh again.

"Of course she knew. She's not new to this game. Look, baby, you're not the first person to have a conniption over the fear of flying, and I'm not the first spouse or significant other to accompany said person on said flight. The staff know what's up. As long as it's not too excessive and it can be kept discrete, they don't really bat too much of an eye. Besides, it's better you get a little stress relief in here than have a nuclear meltdown out there."

Dre absorbed this new information. He found himself surprised, yes, but not actually shocked. He couldn't deny the logic; it was a sound premise. Still, it just seemed so...*bad.*

"So folk just be getting it in in these things, huh?"

"Baby, I know you've heard of the Mile High Club."

"Of course. I just didn't think it was really a *thing* thing. Like, yeah, a few folk have done the tailwind tango..."

Denise stopped stroking and cocked an eye at him.

"Tailwind tango?"

"Yeah," he replied. "'Cause we're on a plane."

She rolled her eyes toward the ceiling.

"And you say I need help."

"Hey," he said defensively, "I'm doing the best I can. It's not like you're leaving me a lot of room to think."

"You're right," she conceded, then proceeded to start stroking him again. "Do continue."

"Thank you," he said, assuming a lofty graciousness. She chose to ignore this. "As I was saying, I know a few folk 'do work,'" this with emphasis, "on a plane, but I didn't think it was an all-the-time thing."

"You'd be amazed at what people get up to on airplanes. They don't call them the friendly skies for nothing." She laughed as Dre shook his head.

"Will wonders never cease. Well," he said, endeavoring to get back on track, "I guess..."

He didn't get to finish because that was the precise moment Denise wrapped her lips around his dick.

Give him the chance, she thought to herself, *and this negro will talk us right into the terminal.* She, however, had other plans.

Pulling him between her soft lips, she sucked him slow but strong, her tongue twirling around and gripping his shaft. With a sigh of peaceful release, he lay his head back against the stall wall. His hands came up to rest on her head, entangling his fingers in her hair. That was one of the other things he loved about her. Of mid-height and petite, Denise was a certified knockout. Honey complected with green eyes, she looked like some Eritrean goddess on extended earthly holiday. She was what they called "slim thick," a slender frame that bottomed out in an absolute bubble. From the front she looked almost tiny, breasts full but not huge, waist trim, hips narrow. But turn her sideways and you'd swear she was trying to smuggle a basketball in her jeans. Her ass was fat, round, and plush, and it fit Dre's large hands perfectly. Atop it all, her hair was a soft, full afro, a crown to crown this woman of elegant royalty. She was his Queen, not just the empty affectation that most folk applied, but truly and completely. She was his lover, his best friend, his help-meet. She was his all and everything, and he loved her with everything he had.

Part of that everything was now lodged down her throat.

Dre lost himself in the sounds and sensations of her ministrations. Keeping her lips soft but tight, she worked his shaft, applying the perfect amount of friction and moisture. While she sucked, she cupped and fondled his sac, reveling in their warm, heavy weight in her hands. Under her expert attention, Dre felt all his anxiety and fear wash warmly away.

Absorbed in bliss, he barely registered her rising from where she'd been tucked on the floor. With deft skill, she maintained suction on his dick as she kicked off her shoes and pulled off her pants. It was only when he felt the shock of cool air on his saliva-slick dick that he noticed she'd changed positions.

Hopping up onto the edge of the counter, she leaned back and spread her legs. With a hungry smile, she patted herself with one hand while beckoning him with the other. Dre smiled as he knelt down and began to oblige her request.

Denise knew how much Dre loved both getting and giving head. Actually, it was possible that he loved the giving more than the getting. He said he was addicted to it: the press of his lips against hers, the sounds she made as he ate, the sweet juiciness when she came for him. Raising her legs to place her heels on his shoulders, she lay back against the mirror and fondled her breasts while she watched and listened to him below.

Dre ate her like a 5 star meal. With relish, he ran his long, thick tongue between her soft, wet lips. Down and around he circled, suckling her plump labia and the pulsing bud between. She moaned as he pushed his tongue inside her, tasting her walls as he drank their ecstasy. He licked her from her clit to her ass crack, causing her to gasp and jump when his tongue penetrated its dark little rosebud. With a sigh and a shudder, she came, savoring the sensations as he licked and sucked her clean.

She opened her eyes to find him staring at her, unadulterated lust radiating like flames from his gaze. She bit her lip in breathless anticipation, then stood and turned, backing into him. His thick, heavy dick rested between her fat, firm cheeks, vibrating in their soft confines.

"You ready, baby," he whispered into her ear, his breath, hot and heavy, shooting shivers through her synapses.

"Yes, daddy," she breathed back, guiding his hands to her waist as she bent over before him. And with a touch and a thrust, he was inside her.

She bit back a moan as he entered her. He was so big that every time they made love she wondered how she'd manage to take it. But manage she did. It seemed like her body had just learned to adjust: she'd get wetter and wetter to accommodate. It's like her body and heart had had a conference and made a mutual decision: we and this man are going to fit.

Dre reveled at the feel of her. Her walls were like a warm, wet vice, crushing his dick in excruciating ecstasy. The experience was always exquisite. He'd never known anybody that fit him so absolutely, so perfectly. It's like she was built for him and he for her. He liked to tell her this in their sweeter, softer moments. Usually she'd laugh and say that he was just saying that because he had to. He'd assure her that he wasn't — and then flip her over to fuck her into insanity to prove his point. She loved it when he proved his points.

Right now he was proving that nothing, not even the fear of falling, flailing, flaming death could stop him from giving his all to his woman. He rammed into her with increasing speed and force, fucking her with articulated alacrity. One thrust sent her up onto her toes, her mouth falling open with a gasp of pure pleasure. The next, even harder and deeper, had her arch until she came completely upright, somehow managing to simultaneously stand up and sit on his dick. Her fat, warm ass pressed back against his hips and thighs as she fought to take all of him. His hands snaked around and wrapped her in their thick embrace, cradling and crushing her as sweetly as her womb did him below.

"Baby, yesss..." she whispered, pushing and plunging back against him. The knuckles on her hands were white from where they gripped the sink so tightly. Her eyelids fluttered and flared, her body shook, her breath came in ragged gasps as he fucked her harder and deeper.

Every inch of Dre's dick was on fire. He felt like he'd been dipped in oil and set alight. The mixture of battling senses, of existential fear and pure, animal lust, formed a concoction unlike any he'd ever experienced. It was like fucking an epiphany. He laughed quietly to himself. Maybe he *did* have a literary dick.

Pulling that train of thought back into its station, he suddenly remembered what they were doing — and where they were doing it.

"Baby," he grunted, sensation and urgency tinting his voice. "I know you said this was kinda normal, but we probably shouldn't be here *too* long, you know?"

"You're...right," Denise squeezed between breaths. "Discretion...is...key." She locked eyes with him in the mirror, her look hungry and lusty. "So that probably means you should go ahead and fuck this nut out of me, huh."

"Mama, you aint said nothing but a word."

And with that, it was on.

With one hand, Dre pushed her over the sink while the other took a grip on her hip, giving him better leverage as his speed and force increased. Denise had put her hands against the mirror and was using them to both maintain her balance and as a brake against which she could push for her *own* leverage. She wasn't just going to take his dick. Oh, no. She was going to give as good as she got.

The small room seemed to rock with the force they were generating. Denise found herself wondering what the load and tolerance specs were for the bolts, welds, and joints holding it together. Yes, a plane was designed to take massive forces and pressure, but the sex they were having was sure to tip somebody's scale somewhere.

Dre drove into her relentlessly, filling her to the brim on every stroke. His fear of flying had been lost as he lost himself inside his woman. He could feel her walls gripping and grabbing him, pulling him in and refusing to let him go. The sweet friction was pushing him closer and closer to his edge, but instead of slowing down to savor it, he sped up, surrendering himself to the plunge. He looked up at the mirror, at them, locked in this raw, sensuous communion. Denise's eyes were screwed tight, passion and pleasure etched across her face, her mouth gaped in silent screams as she took and returned everything he gave. He was fucking her so hard that her ass had turned red, cheeks smacked by their relentless clapping against his thighs. Between and beneath them a pool had formed, Denise's love dripping like a faucet. The sights, sounds, sensations were finally too much.

"Baby," Dre gasped, and Denise felt his hands tighten their grip at the same moment his dick twitched inside her.

"Do it, baby," she moaned back, the shuddering of his shaft sending her up and over. This time, she DID scream, only to be muffled by Dre's massive hand covering her mouth. Pulling her up against him, the heat of their flesh mixing with the scorching flames of their passion fusing them together, they came, thrashing in the throes of the glorious, relentless fire of love.

With a final shudder, they collapsed together onto the sink. Dre lay atop Denise, his breath coming in ragged gasps against her cheek as he fought to slow his racing heart. Denise could feel his dick, still strong and heavy, quivering inside her. She reveled in the sensation, shivering at each little shock. Wiping her forehead, she looked at him through the mirror.

"I don't know about you, but I feel much *much*

better."

Dre laughed, his voice warm, calm, relaxed. Kissing the nape of her neck, he stood. With reluctance, he pulled himself out of her, missing, already, her warm, wet confines. He looked down and shook his head.

"Forget 'discretion;' everybody and they mama is gonna know what's up when I go back out there smelling like a Mr. Marcus video. Hand me some of that soap so I can do something with this."

"Or..." Denise said, grinning wickedly, dropping to her knees again. Dre sighed as she licked him clean: up and down his shaft still shimmering with heat; around the base and through the tangle of his bush; below, to his balls where they hung low and heavy. With a final peck on the tip, Denise smiled and stood.

"See: perfect. Now they won't suspect a thing." Dre smiled at her ruefully.

"Suuuure they won't."

"Hey, if they do, so what? That's the beauty of first class: it comes with certain privileges."

Dre shook his head and chuckled.

"If this is one of those privileges, I might just have to reconsider this whole flying thing."

"Told you," Denise laughed, her voice thrilling through his senses.

They arranged themselves and exited the bathroom, walking back to their seats hand-in-hand. Denise noticed that Dre immediately put his seatbelt on, but this time he at least used the buckle. Hey, progress was progress.

Moments later, their stewardess arrived with the long awaited drink cart. Smiling, she reached inside and pulled out two glasses. She talked while she poured.

"So, are we feeling a bit better?"

Dre grinned at her sheepishly while Denise laughed. With a smile and a gesture of the utmost tenderness, she reached up and over and caressed his cheek. He smiled back, unabashed warmth, love, and appreciation radiant in his eyes.

"I think we've got Killer here calmed down."

"Excellent! We thought you'd be able to get it worked out." Dre thought he detected just a hint of innuendo.

The stewardess stirred their glasses, then dropped citrus wedges into each. She handed them the colorful concoctions with a flourish.

"Here you are, ma'am, sir."

They took the proffered glasses gratefully but curiously. They each took quick sips and then smiled as their tastebuds registered the tart yet sweet flavor followed by the slow punch of good, top shelf liquor. Dre took a bigger sip, then smacked his lips theatrically, causing both Denise and the stewardess to laugh.

"This is some good stuff, definitely better than my Crown and Coke. Out of curiosity, what do you call it?"

The stewardess smiled, a twinkle sparkling in her eye.

"Oh, we call it the Mile High Surprise. It's one of our *specialties...*"

Not for Play-Play
(a poetic interlude)

She caught me as I was walking out to my car, said:

"What's up with all that shit you was talking back there

at the bar?"

And I look around like, who me?

She gon say, "Yeah, you. Talking all that shit bout yo

head is unbeatable and your stroke is dangerous."

"Technically," I said, "my head is impeccable and my

stroke is life changing, but I digress."

She all like, "Yeah, I guess, but we both know you ain't

really bout that life."

And I'm like, did I just get challenged?

Ok.

Cause she don't know yet: Bear is not for play-play.

So I take a step back and appraise the situation.

Now, shorty's ass was hella fat, I'll give her that.

Thighs thick, tits plump, and she swear that pussy on wet-wet.

So I'm like: aight, bet; let's see how this plays out.

So I say, "I don't know what you talmbout, but if you truly doubt me you're than welcome to try to prove me wrong."

And she say -- famous last words -- "Okay, lil daddy; it's on."

So all the way to the crib she talking that good shit.

Talmbout she don't just lick the dick, she gargles that shit, and her ride game will have me tapping out.

And I'm just like, ok; whatever you say.

But be ye warned: Bear is not for play-play.

So we get to the crib and I cut the radio on (got the bluetooth surround so it's linked to the phone)

Cue up the playlist aptly titled "We Finsta Bone," and turn back around and she standing there in nothing but her Y-back thong.

Now, I'ma be honest: thongs is my weakness.

I'm like, "Aight miss, you gon fuck around and catch this peak shit you keep playing with me."

She laughed cause she thought it was a game.

Ok...

Ten minutes later I had her screaming my name so loud the neighbor's dogs started barking --

Cause that's how a Bear marks his gaht damn territory.

See, first I bent her thick ass over and kissed that pussy from the back,

And I'll admit it was rather tasty; she was actually a snack.

And I guess it got too good to her cause she tried to stage a retreat,

But I said, "Nah, shorty, you asked for this. And I'm hungry: let me eat."

Now let me set this record straight: a lotta niggas

"say" they eat, but them niggas don't EAT, ya feel

me?

Niggas be grandma pecking the pussy but I tongue

that bitch down like the head cheerleader on prom

night.

Shit, my head game has given lesbians stage fright.

Y'all thought I was making that shit up in that one

poem, but that shit was for true -- I have references

upon request.

But I digress...

So I'm putting lips to that thang but then slide up in it

with no warning,

And her face lights up like a kid's on Christmas

morning,

Cause after she had came the fifth time she thought

that we was through,

Til I presented her this penis and she said, "Oh, shit;

you brought dick, too?"

You gaht-damn right.

*Now I'm putting this pipe up in her pussy and she can
feel it in her esophagus,*
Got her bucking like a rhinoceros trying to run away.
*Nah, bitch, you asked for this work so you gon get this
work tah-day.*
*My fingernails flexing in the small of her back, and she
arching and squirming like a thick ass cat,*
*And her cat is on hydrate cause it's dripping and
streaming,*
*And she done damn near gone hoarse from all that
shit she been screaming.*

*"Gaht damn, baby!" she say. "Can you give a bitch a
breather?"*
I say "Nope, cause I told yo ass: I got time tah-day."

*And say it with me: Bear is not for muthafuckin play-
play.*

That's when I pulled my dick out and got back down
on my knees,
Licking and sucking and eating the fuzz off that
peach,
And I swear for a minute she forgot how to breathe,
But. That's. What. You. Get. When. You. Fuck-In. With.
Me. *

I got my hands on her hips and hers are locked in my
hair,
And she screaming paint chips off the wall and making
my neighbors scared.
And when I came back up and reintroduced her the
dick,
I swear she cussed out my mama and all her
grandkids.

Now that was actually kinda offensive.
Like, what my mama got to do with this.

That's just rude...

And now I'ma hafta make you pay for that.

*So now I'm back hitting that mufucka, stroking strong,
hard and fast,*
*And she's insulting my upbringing, intelligence and
class.*
*And I slow down for a second, and you can hear the
relief when she gasps --*
Right up until the moment I stick my thumb in her ass.

Oh, yeah; I do that shit, too.

*Reach 'round and playing with her nipples then put my
hand 'round her throat, and she stuttering and
drooling like one of them little baby goats.*
You know that "maaaaaaa" sound they make?

Eyes in the back of her head, pussy gripping my dick,
*And she been stopped speaking English; now she
yelling some foreign shit.*

121

And I'm hitting angles, smacking ass, squeezing hips;

Flipped her over, biting nipples, licking ears, sucking lips.

I put her ass through her paces, did some shit she never tried.

I fucked her on the floor and on the table and on the back of my neighbor's ride.

I fucked that chick for an hour without breaking my stroke,

Til she got stuck in that last position; shit, I thought that bitch broke.

Now she laying there trembling, breathing hard and shit, toes curled up like they throwing gang signs, pieces of my sheets stuck in her fingernails, and her pussy is doing that fish out of water thing they do, and she say,

"Gaht damn, baby, I didn't believe it, but all that shit you said was true."

I said "I'm glad you realize -- now get yo ass ready for

round two."

Cause I heard somebody say: Bear is not for muthafuckin play-play.

*Yes, that was a Tank reference. If you know, you know.

Tomboys

"Ha! Got you, nigga. Get that weak shit outta here!" She jumped up, waving the controller as Kobe dropped a tomahawk dunk on King James.

"Yeah, whatever, nigga. You just lucky my finger slipped on that fade-away."

"Fade away on these nuts, nigga!" she laughed, driving the lane again. They both laughed, settling further into the game.

Several minutes and flashy dunks later, the game was over. Resting between restarts, she stood and stretched.

"Yo, J, I'm finna grab a beer. You want one?"

"Fa sho," he responded, watching her go. He noticed how the loose, gray sweats still managed to hug her thick thighs and hips, and how full her sports bra was beneath her favorite jersey.

She came back and handed him a bottle, then

took a swig of her own.

"Yo, you want some of this tree? Demarion be selling that GAS gas."

He nodded and watched her roll the blunt. He couldn't help but linger on her full lips as they expertly licked the edges and worked the roll. It reminded him of how she licked his dick. He grinned inwardly and wickedly at the thought.

He and Shae had known each other since middle school. They'd met in gym during the first week of school, both picked for the same squad of a 21 pick-up game. He and the other dudes had grumbled about her inclusion until they saw the way she handled the ball and drove the lane against guys near twice her size. She was small but lithe, strong and quick, with a mouth and wit to match. She kept up with both the game and the trash talk and immediately became a regular teammate and fast friend. They'd spent many afternoons at his house playing 2K and many others at hers shooting on the hoop in her backyard. Because of her tomboyish dress and mannerisms, their friends and family saw them as almost brother and sister, two best and inseparable friends. It was a façade that they made a point to maintain, because if truth had been known...

Shae lit the blunt and took a deep drag. She held the smoke in her lungs for several seconds, then exhaled the cloud before immediately pulling it back in through her nostrils. He laughed at the ritual. She hit him on the shoulder and passed him the blunt.

"What you over there kee-kee'ing about, lil nigga."

"You smoke like a whole ass nigga. I swear sometimes that you a dude in disguise."

She cut her eyes at him and smirked.

"Oh, so I guess that makes you gay, cause you sho like being up in this 'dude's' guts." She looked down at his lap where his dick had unmistakably started to rise inside his shorts. The truth was impossible to hide.

To anyone looking in, the conversation would have seemed like sacrilege. Not only were the two so close as to be twins, but, by all appearances, Shae was one of the boys — with all that came with it. She wore baggy jeans and J's, kept her long hair in cornrows or basic ponytails and never wore makeup. She balled with the fellas, cursed harder than most of them, and could hit a joint or a bottle with the best. Most guys had long since written her off as a lesbian and just another one of the homies. And she didn't try to dissuade the thought. Even though they'd never actually seen her with other females, let alone a girlfriend, they'd never seen her date a guy or open herself up to be approached, so made and ran with the assumption. The one time they'd been inclined to rethink things was Senior Prom. That night she took everybody off guard and left more than a few speechless. Hair curled and coifed, face beat to the gawds, she'd stepped out in a banging red dress and stilettos. The dress showed off every last inch of her curves, and there were a lot of inches and a lot of curves. "Gaht dayumn," their homeboy Marcus had said. "All this time you been playing basketball, we ain't know you was SITTING on one." She and J — her date for the evening — had laughed it off before she cussed Marcus like a sailor on shore leave. And just that fast, she was one of the boys again.

Yep, she was one of the boys, J thought. She was his homie, his bestie, his boy — and the best pussy he'd ever had.

Taking a hit from the perfectly rolled blunt, he returned to the conversation and waved the insinuation off. "Whatever, bro," he said through a lungful of smoke. "Don't be tryna get all big headed."

"Oh, you wanted to give me some head?" she said all feigned innocence. "All you had to do was say so."

He turned, ready to flame her with a joke, but stopped as he watched her stand and then pull down her sweats. He stared at the black thong fighting to hold onto her hips and the fat pussy between her thighs.

"Bruh, you play all day," he said rolling his eyes, but not before she caught him licking his lips in anticipation.

"Um, did you have something better to do? Ain't like you was actually winning."

"Whatever, nigga," he said, pushing her back on the couch and grabbing a hold of her thighs. "Just be lucky I like you."

She sighed as his hands pulled the taut and already wet fabric to the side and moaned as she felt the first pass of his tongue over her swollen clit.

"Yeah, you like me, but you love this pussy."

And he did. For all their back and forth, the play fights and the hooping and the brother/sister camaraderie and vibes, he had never come across anyone as good as her. And she knew it. They knew about all of each other's experiences, as best friends do. They'd told each other after each had lost their virginities, discussed the most intimate details of the experience with those and subsequent partners. Shae had always messed with guys from other schools, dudes who were both distant and discreet, so no word had ever filtered back to their circle. Besides, both of their body counts were low, neither really interested in rando's for rando's sake. And when they finally hooked up, everybody else was immediately pushed off the table. She was, indeed, the best he'd ever had, and if he was being completely honest, she was the best he ever wanted to have. Not that he'd tell her that, of course.

"Aye, nigga," she said, snapping him out of his reverie, "you gon think or you gon eat? This pussy aint gon kiss itself."

He rolled his eyes and smacked her on her ample ass.

"Bruh, stfu and let me do what I'm doing. All this talking, knowing full well I'm finna have you screaming like a mufucka."

"Yeah, yeah, nigga..." she started, but immediately succumbed to a moan as his tongue found her favorite spot and went to work. They were so close that they knew each other inside and out — literally. He'd learned all of her favorite spots and positions, and had become an expert at working each and every one.

Her hands gripped the back of his head as his lips dipped deeper between hers. He licked and nibbled and sucked at her lips and clit, alternating long and deep probes with faster and stronger flicks. He wrapped his lips around her pearl and suckled it gently, his tongue caressing the sensitive tip, sending her into shudders of pleasure. When she came, her thighs clamped against his head as he lapped her cum from the top of her pussy to the crack of her ass. Knowing her, he immediately slid a finger inside her, finding and massaging her g-spot as his tongue licked circles around her clit. She immediately came again, arching her back and screaming, her strong thighs

132

damn near crushing him in her ecstasy.

"Damn, lil bihh, lighten up," his muffled voice rose from between her legs. "You tryna decapitate a nigga?" They both laughed as she relaxed her vise grip, her legs falling to the couch, trembling slightly still with the resonating aftershocks.

"Shit, don't be mad at me," she replied, stretching her arms high above her head, a gesture of full and deep satisfaction. "You the one did it." She looked down at him and smirked. "And 'decapitate,' my nigga? You trying out some new big words?"

"Shi, I don't know about big words, but I do got sumn big for you." And with that he stood and dropped his shorts. Looking down at her, he saw a look in her eye he knew all too well. He smiled to himself as she leaned forward and grabbed his dick, her hands expertly massaging him to his full, throbbing length.

"Oh, so all this is for me, lil daddy?" With one hand she gripped the base of his shaft while the other stroked it up and down.

"You already know."

"And it's all mine?" she teased, now stroking the frill at the base of the head where she knew he was the most sensitive. She was rewarded with the feeling of his legs quivering and a shiny drop of pre cum glistening at his tip.

"I mean, I'on't know about 'all.' There is that one bird Stacy..." However, he couldn't finish because she'd just taken him fully into her mouth and into the back of her throat. He groaned and sank back onto the couch. Shae followed him down and around, coming to rest on her knees between his legs in prime dick-sucking position. She pulled his dick from her lips for a second, the shaft dark and glistening with her saliva.

"Umm, who this bitch Stacy?" she said feigning anger, cupping his balls while licking the underside of his head. J, his head back against the couch and his eyes closed, muttered almost incoherently.

"Huh?"

"If you can 'huh' you can hear." She slid his head between her lips again while stroking his shaft, causing him to moan and grab the back of her head. She pulled away and asked again.

"I said: who this bitch Stacy?"

He looked down at her, an almost pained expression in his eyes. She was working him perfectly, her hands, lips and tongue doing everything she knew he liked. He was finding it hard to concentrate.

"Man, I was just kidding," he said, reaching for her head again, urging her to continue. She shook him off, though, continuing both her line of questioning and her machinations on his dick.

"Oh, so now you kidding."

"Yes, woman, I was just kidding." He shuddered as she hit him with the double-hand twist and then lapped up the ensuing stream of pre cum dripping down her fingers.

"So this IS my dick?" she said, running her

tongue up his shaft to the soft and sensitive spot beneath the head.

"Yeah, man," he stammered, eyes pleading as he watched her wrap her plush lips around him and suck gently.

"Then gon say it, lil nigga." She raised his shaft and licked his balls, causing him to grip the couch from the sudden sensation.

"It's your dick, man, aight."

"Say it like you mean it," she said, now nuzzling and sucking his balls as her hands gripped and stroked his length, pushing him perilously close to a nut.

"It's your dick, damn," he said, trying to keep up with the conversation while the world behind his eyelids exploded in fireworks and sparklers as she worked him toward what promised to be a phenomenal climax

"Say it with your chest, lil nigga!"

He opened his mouth to clown her for such an

136

inappropriate reference, but found that he couldn't breathe as she'd just shoved his dick all the way down her throat and was milking him with it while simultaneously lapping and licking his balls. He came so hard he thought he'd pass out, jet after jet of cum exploding into her esophagus as she sucked and swallowed him unmercifully.

Finally he pushed her off, reaching that point of sensitivity that was impossible for any man to stand. She laughed as he lay back, panting, arms thrown to his sides, looking fully and completely spent.

"You need a towel, my nigga?" she asked, still stroking him firmly but gently, coaxing him back to life. "Look like you broke a little sweat, there."

"Man, fuck you." They laughed as he collected himself, she placing light kisses along his shaft and against the head as he rose back to attention.

"I'm just saying you look a little wore out. Looking like a lightweight in these streets, my G."

"Man, fuck you," he said again, laughing.

"That's the second time you've said that shit. Don't talk about it, my nigga; be about it." And with that she stood, removed her thong, jersey and bra, and straddled him, taking him inside her in one long, slow motion. They both moaned as her strong interior muscles gripped his length, he throbbing in response inside her. He reached around and grabbed her fat ass as she began to bounce and grind against him.

"You want me to be about it, lil baby?" he asked, pulling her down and into him harder. She arched her back and closed her eyes as she reached forward and grabbed his shoulders.

"Yes, daddy."

He leaned forward and kissed her collarbone.

"What you say, lil baby?" he asked, hands gripping and squeezing her hips.

"I said yes, daddy." She shivered as she felt him pushing even deeper into her.

"Oh, so we off that 'lil nigga' shit, huh?" he asked, sucking and biting the soft flesh of her throat.

She sat up and popped him in the head.

"Nigga, is you gon joke or fuck me, cause a nigga tryna get this nut." He laughed at her sudden vehemence.

"I swear you a whole ass nigga." She started to retort until he leaned forward and pulled one of her nipples into his mouth. "And I mean that metaphorically." She let out a gasp and shook at the sudden shock of sensation.

"Metaphorically, metaphysically, meta-whatever nigga; just fuck me."

And he did.

He sucked and licked her nipples as she rode him, her pussy tight and wet and hot around him. His hands gripped her ass, her back, her thighs, guiding her in a rhythm they'd developed and perfected over many sessions. When he licked the skin over her heart, she moaned. When he bit her nipples, she shuddered. And when he grabbed her braids, forcing her head back as he slammed up into her, she screamed and came.

She leaned against him, fighting to catch her breath as shimmering spasms rippled through the walls of her pussy. She was about to climb off of him when he stopped her. Sliding his hands up and under her thighs, he gripped the firm flesh of her ass and stood. She moaned deep as he slid deeper into her. Looking into her eyes, he carried her across the room and placed her back against the wall. She wrapped her arms around his neck and her legs around his waist to give them both better purchase. She bit him playfully on the lips as her knees rose, allowing him greater access.

"Oh, so you tryna pull out some tricks on a bitch?"

"You keep talking all this shyt so I had to remind you who was running thangs in here."

Her eyes opened in mock confusion as she looked over his shoulders and around the room.

"Running?" she said, then shivered as his lips

140

found and nipped her neck. "Who running?"

"Man, you know yo ass be on that Sprint Cup," he laughed, licking up the curve of her throat and to her ear. She sighed and grabbed the back of his head as his tongue played against the lobe. They could both feel her getting wetter and tighter by the second.

"Nah, my nigga, that's you." She leaned forward and bit *his* ear, causing him to shudder and his dick to twitch within her. She pulled back and laughed at his reaction, the sound deep and husky with her desire. "You be on yo Usain Bolt in this bihh."

"Oh, so that's what we on?" he asked, tightening his grip on her ass, palming it like the basketball it resembled.

"You already know," she responded, pulling him close, their bodies fusing, breath mingling from lips a hair's breadth apart, hearts beating in perfect rhythm and harmony.

"Then let's see who running now," he replied, and thrust himself in her to the hilt, filling and stretching her to the limit as she screamed out in a cascade of ecstasy.

Positioning her so that her shoulders were pinned to the wall, he angled himself so that he could pull her ass down and into him with each stroke. In this way, she was completely at his mercy, a fact he took full advantage of. Setting his rhythm fast and deep, he fucked her into submission. He slid her up and down and along his dick, changing angles and speed with practiced precision. He knew all her spots and was making a point to hit every one. Head thrown back, eyes squeezed tight, chest heaving as she fought for breath, she struggled to keep up. Her pride wouldn't just let him get the best of her, but he was so gaht damned good that she was losing the battle.

He shifted his grip on her slightly, and instead of the respite she expected, she found herself instead in a new and fiercer predicament. Adjusting his angle for leverage, he forced her legs up and onto his shoulders. As though it weren't impossible, he was

142

now even deeper inside her, hitting what she swore was the very back of her throat. She immediately came, her lust spraying from her in a glistening rain as she squirted around his dick.

"Oh, we done cut the faucets on in this ho, huh?" he laughed, adjusting his rhythm to hit that spot again and harder.

"Nigga," she gasped, each word fighting past the shocks slamming through her body, causing her breath to come out in ragged gasps, "you talk...a lotta...shyt."

"Do sumn about it, then," he laughed back, his eyes glinting in mischief and lust.

"Bet," she said, shifting her weight and grip. The challenge had been made and accepted, and she wasn't about to lose.

Grabbing his head, she pulled him closer and stuck her tongue down his throat, something she knew he loved. As she swirled inside his mouth, her hips swirled along his dick. Locking both her hands and her

143

heels behind his head, she took control, fucking him back as ferociously as he'd fucked her. Up and down him she bounced, contracting the muscles in her walls on every upstroke, gripping and squeezing him relentlessly. He twitched and thumped inside her, every nerve on every inch of his dick responding to her ministrations. She knew him as well and he knew her, knew every angle that made his breath quicken, the exact speed to make his pulse race, the exact spots that made his knees buckle. She knew every last inch of him, and she was going to fuck them all.

"Baby, slow down," he muttered against her neck, his breath coming hard and heavy against her flesh.

"Nah, lil nigga," she breathed, her voice husky and thick as she bit his ear and then dug her nails into the soft yet taut skin of his shoulders and back. The sensation made his whole body shudder and she felt his dick grow almost double inside her. "You was talking all that shit a minute ago. Where you at now?"

"Man, fuck you," he groaned, tightening his grip on her fat, plush ass, fighting the rising tide boiling up his dick. In response, her pussy clamped down harder, a sure sign telling them both that they were moments away from release.

"Okay," she responded, and in one smooth motion, she rose all the way up on his dick, arcing herself to his very apex, and then crashed back onto him, driving him home to the deepest, tightest, wettest spot yet. The sensation was too much, and they exploded simultaneously, literally, she gushing what seemed like buckets while he blasted shot after shot inside her. The feel of the other's orgasm amplified their own, expanding and prolonging the sensation until it seemed that they had been and would cum forever.

Finally, breathless, spent and drained, they collapsed in a sweaty, sticky heap.

As they lay there, her head resting against his chest, his fingers drawing lazy circles against her ass, they basked in the afterglow of their session and something else, something less definable but no less real. Neither would admit it — ironically because that would break "bro code" — but theirs was something deeper. Deeper than friends, deeper than homies, deeper, even than family, theirs was a bond true and unshakable. They were soulmates, pure and simple — though they'd probably beat the ass of anybody that suggested it.

Finally, Shae sat up and stretched. Looking up at her, at her flat stomach curving into the crown of her breasts, and her narrow waist flaring out into her ample hips, J felt himself stiffen. Shae pretended not to notice as she climbed off of him and stood, turning slightly and arching her back so he could see her perfectly poised in sexy silhouette. She turned back and reached down to slap him on the thigh.

"Good job, my nigga. You got a decent stroke on you." She laughed and dodged as he threw his shorts at her.

"Bruh!" he laughed, looking for something else to toss. "Why you always gotta be so niggerish?" She turned back and popped him again.

"Cause you my nigga." She paused. "You *are* my nigga, right?" He couldn't help noticing the emphasis she placed on the word, but just in case he missed it, her hand once again on his dick spoke volumes.

"You already know, shorty. You my nigga if you don't get no bigger." They laughed and she turned toward the kitchen.

"Yo, I'ma grab a Gatorade; you want one?"

"Fa sho," he called, craning his neck around to watch her go. Watching her ass bounce and flex with every step made his dick stiffen even more. When she came back and handed him his drink, she took a look at it then reached down and slapped it lightly and playfully.

"Let me find out my nigga tryna do rounds!" She laughed, eyeing him, a renewed glint of lust in her

147

eyes. In answer, he sat up, grabbed her by the waist, turned her around and bent her over the couch. She spread her legs and arched her back, moaning as he slid into her again.

"I'ma show yo' ass 'rounds," he said, grabbing her hips and setting his stroke. "Oh, and while we here: tf you mean 'say it with your chest?' See, what we *not* gon do..."

My Homeboy's Girl

I am fucking my homeboy's girl. I can't get that fact out of my mind. Try as I might, much as I'm trying to ignore it, I just can't stop thinking it: I am fucking my homeboy's girl.

And I am FUCKING my homeboy's girl. I'm dicking this bitch down like dick is about to go out of style. She's screaming so loud the neighbors' dogs just started barking; I'm legit afraid that somebody is gonna call the cops. She's ripping sheets off my bed, tossing pillows, threatening to crack the frame. Her ass is high and in serious motion, taking my thrusts like a jet engine piston and giving back as good as she's getting. She's already come five times and from the look and sound of things she's trying to get at least five more. All in all, it cannot not be denied: I am seriously fucking my homeboy's girl.

And I hadn't meant to.

My homebody Mike is on a bid upstate. He was sentenced three months ago to a three year stretch on a strike three behind some stupid shit. Mike is my boy, but nobody would say he's the sharpest spoon in the drawer. And, technically, Mike is my "boy," but not my *boy*. Sure, we'd all grown up together down in South Dallas: me, Mike, Rayshawn, Lou-Lou and the rest. We ran together, hooped together, chilled together and hoed together. But though I "know" them niggas, they aint my BOYS boys. They just my homeboys, which is different. At least that's what I keep telling myself as I fuck my homeboy's girl.

Sharice had always had an eye for me. Even back in high school and up into college — we being two of the very few to actually go — I knew she was clocking me. But I wasn't interested. Yeah, she was fine and all. Slight correction, there: shorty was fine af. Even as a teenager she had one of those shapes grown women make trips south of the border to buy.

All the girls in our school wore tight khakis and polos as part of their uniforms, tryna show off what little shapes they had, but Sharice was the kinda chick who bought what should have been loose but ended up tight anyway. That little mufucka was FINE fine. Never topping 5'2", she had to be pushing at least 180 pounds, and it all sat incredibly right on her frame. Every nigga we knew had been trying to get at her for as long as any of us could remember but she shaded them all. Her mama is a known ho (shorty had like 8 brothers and sisters from 10 different niggas; try to figure that shit out), and the rest of the fam wasn't too much better. So Sharice was the good girl of the bunch. And she was a legit good girl. Focused in school, had aspirations and goals, a model of one of the ones that would make it out. And then she met Mike. Fucking Mike. It was a train wreck waiting to happen, made worse because absolutely everyone saw it coming but her. Speaking of coming, she was doing it again.

151

"Daddy, ooh daddy, oooooh daddy! Fuck!" she's screaming, arching up and throwing herself back against me. Her unconscionably fat ass is doing stripper tricks like she hit a lick, and I'm sitting back and enjoying the view. My dick is super strong and long inside of her, covered with a shit ton of her cum that's dripping off of my nuts and her lips onto a rather sizable puddle on my sheets. "Daddy, why the fuck are you fucking me like this?"

"Shit, bitch, 'cause you asked me to."

I waited for a reply but she was screaming again. As I absorbed the echoes, I had to admit that it was a good question. Why AM I fucking her like this?

It was probably the way she came over, tears in her eyes, heartbroken over what had gone down between her and Mike. Exactly three days ago, exactly three months into his bid, another girl had come to her house and told her that she was pregnant. When Sharice, in tears, called this nigga for answers — ON THE PHONE SHE WAS PAYING FOR — he just shrugged and said, "I mean, but are you really mad, tho?" This muthafucka Mike. Sigh.

So to my house she came, eyes full of tears, heart full of pain, and jeans full of one of the fattest asses I have ever seen in my life.

Let me attempt to make this explicitly clear: when I say that mufucka is fat, I don't mean just big. I don't mean just round. I don't mean just plump and hippy and with some heft to it. I mean that mufucka is FAT. Mufucka so fat you could put your arm around her waist, let go your hand, and that mufucka'd just rest there. Mufucka so fat I swear fo' gawd you could sit a small child back there. Mufucka so fat I've seen older church ladies be tempted to foreswear Jesus when she walks past. I repeat: that mufucka is FAT.

And I like fat asses, so here we are.

I'm dicking this bitch like there's no tomorrow, 'cause the awareness I still maintain is telling me there just might not be. See, Mike has some brothers, and those brothers are not what you'd call well-wrapped

153

individuals. Mike's brothers are what you could call "touched." Mike's brothers are what the old folks just flat out say are crazy af. You know it's bad when old black folks just cut to the chase. Them niggas scare everybody, and sometimes I think they scare each other. Mike is the baby — if you could call anybody that stupendously fucked up a baby — and his brothers are all extremely protective. It's probably because they basically had to raise each other when their daddy skipped town and their mama was locked up on a 20 year stretch for murdering her way to the top of the local drug empire. You see what kinda family we're working with here? In any event, Mike's brothers are what could be called at the most genteel of times "trouble," and if wind got to them that I was peeling paint off the wall with their brother's girl, well, there'd be some slow singing and flower bringing around my part of town.

Sharice screams again, clenches, shudders and proceeds to squirt all over me. "Great," I'm thinking, looking down at my drenched jeans, "and this is why you take your pants off." I smack her ass as she starts to come down and kick my stroke into another gear. Regardless of my obvious reservations, I'm gon fuck this chick like she owes me money. Come to think of it, that nigga Mike owes me money.

So back to the story. Shorty had come to my house, crying, snotting, booing all the hoo about this nigga Mike, and of course I try to be the good nigga and console her. I'm sitting on the bed next to her, arm wrapped around her shoulders in what I knew was the perfect brotherly way, and tried not to stare down at her perfectly un-sisterly tits straining the fuck out of her shirt. Shaking my head to clear the excessively graphic visions I was getting, I rubbed her back.

"I mean, you knew that nigga was a ho, right?" I said with all the sympathy I'd learned to muster.

Yup, I actually said that.

Okay, I'm more book smart than life smart. Sue me.

"But why, thooo? I mean, I did everything for him. I gave him a place to stay, bought him all the J's, even bought him a new Playstation when he broke mine. And I even did stuff *with* him." At this my ears perked up. Was this going where I thought it was going?

"What you mean," I asked her, gently patting her shoulder and trying not to let her see the freaky ass hopeful glint that had come into my eyes.

"I mean, we did EVERYthing. I let him come on my face." Uh huh. "In my mouth." Is that right? "In my ass." Lawd, I think I just fainted a little bit. "And when he said he wanted to try with other people..." She started crying again and so did I.

Mutha. Fucking. Mike.

I aint shit. I'm just gon be honest about that. I aint in any form, fashion, or function shit. This girl was sitting here crying her life away, coming to me as a friend and confidant and a shoulder and a help, and all I could think about was pushing her legs back and trying to decipher the names of those bitches she'd fucked through mouth-to-monkey divination. Lawd, sometimes I'm ashamed of me.

"There there," I said, awkwardly patting her shoulder as she collapsed into my chest. There there? Nigga, who tf says "there there?" A nigga trying to keep his dick from jumping up and hitting this bitch in the chin is who. Things were going south fast, and I was not in a rational state of mind.

"It's okay, shorty. I mean, it's not 'okay;' that was some real fucked up shit." Cue fresh stream of tears. I had to be the worst Hallmark movie ever known to man. But I plowed ahead. "It could be worse, if you think about it. Fact is, now you know, and that means you can move on with your life and find something and somebody better." I was actually proud of myself for that last part. Take that, emotional obliviousness. I had just given this woman the obligatory ray of hope that always makes things better and I was sure that somewhere a ghetto angel had just won his wings.

She looked up at me, tearful hope in her eyes.

"You really think so?"

"Fa sho I do, shorty. I mean, any nigga would be crazy lucky to have you. Matter fact..."

That was as far as I got before she rammed her tongue down my throat. Annnnnd Houston we have a wrap.

Nigga, my brain shut the entire fuck down. I forgot the situation, Mike, his brothers. Hell, for a moment I forgot my own gaht damn name. She was stripping her clothes off and I was trying not to rip them bitches. Her shirt came off first and then her bra, and when I tell you them mufuckas was sumn serious? You remember in Coming to America when Arsenio Hall's character said old girl had breasts like cassava melons? Well, I looked up cassava melons once, and gaht damn if this bitch wasn't from Zamunda. I buried my face in them mufuckas and sucked like I'd just come out the womb. Lawd this bitch got some

158

amazing ass titties. Just soft and heavy and nipples thick and long. I probably would and could have spent the rest of my day right there, happily mouthing those melon-ous mounds, but then she reached down my jeans and grabbed my dick and my brain reset itself and said, "But wait: there's more!"

Before I knew it she had my pants around my ankles and my dick down her throat. And when I say "down her throat," that is NOT a euphemism. No, my dick was literally down her throat. And I got a big dick. I aint tryna brag, but if I whip this shit out, the room might get dark. I'm heavy structured, big boned, hung low — some of y'all will catch that reference later. However he said it, my shit is prodigiously endowed, and right now it was prodigiously endowing her esophagus.

You know what: I ain't lied yet so I ain't gon start now. Shorty brought the bitch out of me. Deadass. She brought the complete and utter bitch out of me. The things she did with her mouth...whoo,

159

lawd. Not only did she inhale that mufucka, she stuck out her tongue and licked my nuts while she did it. When I tell you I thought I was gonna choke the bitch from the inside... Aint nobody ever done that shit before. Hell, I didn't know that shit was doable. I do know, however, that I'ma find every bitch in the country that CAN do it and I'm moving them hoes to a commune. Congratulations, bitches: you're now sister wives.

Family, she sucked my dick up till she hiccuped. I'm laying there trying not to cry too openly or loudly because I'm having a legit out of body experience. I was out of my body and so deep down hers I started wondering if it really was possible to get a chick pregnant from head like our parents always tried to scare us with. If it was, welp, congratulations mama: I's the pappy now.

I'm laying there, bedsheets stuck all up in my butt crack from where I been clenching and scooting so hard, and she stand up and wipes her chin (licking her fingers thereafter) and asks me if I was done. I could only look at her in silent awe, which I guess she took as an affirmative "no" cause she proceeded to unbutton her pants and pull them mufuckas off. And Lawd. Dear Lawd. Sweet father, holy Lawd. When I say that THEE fattest, wettest, furriest muthafuckin monkey was just staring at me eye to eye. I swear that mufucka sneered at me. That mufucka challenged me. That mufucka called me a dirty name. Swear I heard it call me a bitch.

I aint gon be too many muthafuckas, now, ya hear.

I grabbed her hips, spun her around to the bed, pushed her down, and put my face in that thang so deep it was like I was bobbing for last years apples. Nigga, I ate that bitch til I literally got full, I shit you not. Shit, I was so deep in it I think I licked her belly button. You ever ate a pussy so good it had you thinking some deep, philosophical shit? Nigga, I'm eating that shit and started revisiting scripture. I'm sitting there going, what if Adam didn't eat an apple, but a peach? I was literally trying to work out the ramifications. That would definitely put more emphasis on Adam's response when God showed up ("It was that woman you gave me"). Bruh, I ate that pussy til my tongue hurt, and I kept eating it til it stopped. I ain't never second-winded my tongue before, but this was a day for a host of first-evers.

I'm on my seventeenth helping of pussy when she grabs my wrists and pulls me up and on top of her.

"I need that dick, daddy," she whispers up at me, looking deep into my eyes with what I could only describe as the Nala effect. You remember that scene from the Lion King when you swear if there was an adult version Nala just told Simba that she wanted him to Hakuna her Tatas? Yup, that's the one. My dick jumped so hard I hit myself in the stomach. Disney knew what they were doing.

I'm still tryna play things cool — for what,

right? — because this still is, after all, my homeboy's girl. Yes I had just fucked her windpipe like I was tryna tickle her uterus from the other side, and yes I had just eaten her out like a 1930's stereotype at a Watermelon festival, but fucking, actually fucking, was a different matter. I wanted to be sure she was cool before we crossed an un-recrossable line.

"You sure, mama? I mean, if you good, I'm good."

"Oh, I'm good, daddy. I'm real good." My naive ass just thought she meant she was okay — right up till she grabbed my dick and shoved it between her lips. Turns out, she was not referring to her state of mind but rather her state of vagine. And as the lord said at the moment of creation: it was good.

Shorty fit me like she was made for me. She gripped me so tight I thought she'd rub the skin off, but she was so wet I was afraid to slide back too far for fear of shooting across the room. Shit had me in a metaphysical quandary — there I go thinking deep shit again — and I was at a loss for words. I literally lost the power of speech a moment later when she grabbed one of her tits and stuck her nipple in her mouth. Okay. I'm back. I have regained clarity and focus, and first order of business is blowing this bitch's back out.

I dipped my head to suck the other nipple, for which she sighed and grabbed the back of my neck. I flicked my tongue against it, circling and teasing, then blew on it lightly so it would stiffen. She moaned and arched her back and offered me the other one. I repeated the process making both rise like — I was gonna say monuments or soldiers or some other poetic cliché shit like that, but at the moment I was too busy fucking to think of anything that nice. However you put it, them mufuckas was high and tight. What else was high was my dick, and what was tight was her pussy that she was currently milking me with.

She raised those thick, magnificent thighs, and

164

for a moment I thought she was spreading to offer me better passage, but then she kept tilting them back and toward the bed. She opened her eyes, grabbed my hands, and placed them on the back of her ankles.

"Fuck me, daddy," she said to me, biting her full lips in what I read as ecstatic expectation. "Fuck this fucking pussy."

I'm a devout feminist and I believe it's a good man's job to comply to a good woman's wishes.

Yeah, that's the shit I'm going with.

Nigga, when I tell you I tried to put a new hole in that mufucka? I was stroking so hard I thought I hit her spine at one point. This, apparently, was her spot, and it also, apparently, wasn't a spot that Mike could hit often. I'm ashamed of the fact that I know this. I'm even more ashamed that my neighbors apparently know it now, too.

I fucked that chick for what seemed like an eternity. Actually couldn't have been more than 35, 45 minutes, 52 if I'm being generous. Whole time she's giving as good as she's getting, squirming, sliding, matching me stroke for stroke, and wetting my bed so much I could hear the springs squish. I honestly didn't know a chick could cum that much. I was scared she'd dehydrate. Apparently, tho, fat booty bitches carry extra liquid reserves like camels in the Sahara. Look at me learning new things today.

Finally, I had to call a timeout. I'm good at what I do, a master of mind over body, but her body was so damn good I was ready to hand over ownership.

"Baby, I'm finna cum." I tried to say this in as manly a way as possible, but I don't know if there is a manly way to say that. The fact that my voice tremored while I said it probably didn't help matters.

"You gonna cum for me, daddy?" she whispered up at me. Bitch, didn't I just say that? Look, I'm not tryna be disrespectful, but when a nigga says that phrase, he got a specific number of strokes left before it's all systems go, and saying shit like that cuts those strokes almost in half. I had a good 7-8 pumps left when I asked that question, and suddenly I'm down to three.

"You gonna cum for me, daddy," she said again, and next, not a question but a statement: "Cum for me, daddy."

Okay.

I stiffen up like I'm bout to have a fucking seizure because I can tell this is about to be the big one. Call Fred Sanford cause I'm bout to join him and Elizabeth. Oh, I thought that one from head was serious? This shit threatened to be record breaking. I was actually almost legit scared. Can you break a nigga from a nut too strong? What if my system actually shut down? What if I got locked in my O-position forever? Do niggas in that state get to go to a special facility? Would my insurance cover that?

I'm thinking these things as I'm stroking to my last stroke, and suddenly she's not there anymore. I am perplexed. One second I'm knee deep in Shangri

La, the next I'm swinging in air — and then, suddenly, I'm back down her throat. I literally blacked out for like 5 seconds.

I need a moment to reflect on that.

...

...

...

Okay, I'm back.

So I'm collapsed on the bed, facedown, trying to evaluate my life and what I did to deserve what I have come to believe is a personal test of my will and fortitude when I hear a noise beside me and look over to find her two fingers deep in that thang and going to town.

"Bitch...are you still...ready?" I was astonished and aghast. This bitch had fucked me into weight loss, and she's still wet and willing.

"It was just so good, daddy, I can't stop. I'm just so fucking wet," and with that she pulled her fingers out from between her lips and put them between mine.

Lo and behold me and my dick are back in business.

I rolled over onto my back, still licking her fingers and pulled her over and on top of me. She started to straddle my hips, but I grabbed her ass and turned her instead. She smiled and straddled my face. I wrapped my arms around her waist and my lips around her clit as she slid me back down her throat. We ate and sucked each other for what seemed like another eternity. At this point I had given up all attempts to ascribe to any concept of time. We out here in the cosmos, baby, testing out Einstein's theories of relativity. E equals eat this bitch til she faints. Time, nigga? I got alllll the time tah-day. Tired? Bitch, I don't get tired.

With a final slurp, she extricated my elongation from her esophagus, flipped around and straddled my legs.

"You gon fuck me again, daddy?"

In answer I grabbed her hips, tilted mine, and

169

slid up and into her. She arched her back and moaned as I found my way home.

"Yup, for as long and as much as you need."

Famous last words.

She rode me like she was a certified equestrian, and I swear I ain't never seen a horse in the hood that wasn't under the hood of a Chevy. She'd alternate between leaning forward so I could squeeze and suck her tits, and sitting back and up, grinding her hips in circles as she took my shaft to the hilt. I lay back watching her, her eyes closed, mouth slightly parted, hands cupping her breasts and playing with her nipples, and for the first time in my life I thought about what love looked like. Yes, we were just fucking, and yes, this was still my homeboy's girl, but in the midst of it all we were two people that had found a true and genuine connection, two people that had known each other for years, forming a bond that neither of us recognized, but that was true and real and steadfast. We were two bodies but one mind, joined together in the oldest and purest and most sacred way. It, and she, was a thing of beauty.

I held that thought right up till she pulled her legs up, got into a squat, and proceeded to do it with no hands.

I'd tell you what happened next but I think I blacked out again.

Fellas, real talk, if you aint never had a super thick, super pretty, big booty bitch pull a Meg Thee Stallion on your dick, you, my good man, are missing all the way out. Sadly, that's about 99% of the population. It's lamentable, really — but fuck y'all; I got mine.

And I was about to get mine again.

"Umm, baby?" I stammered, trying to grab her hips and slow her down.

"Yes, daddy?" she moaned, eyes still closed, back still arched, ass still trying to exorcise the demons of my dick.

"I'ma..." and before I could finish, she hopped

off. Does this bitch have telepathy? Is she reading my mind? Is she reading my soul? Is she actually reading my dick? What is this sorcery? But before I could explore the scientific and psychometric ramifications of super-human exogenesis further — Google it — I realized that she'd not given me respite but redirection. She'd hopped up on the bed beside me, thighs spread, ass tooted and was looking over at me expectantly.

"Sooo, is you cumming or nah?"

My answer: or nah.

See, backshots is my shit. I am the master of the backshot. Shit, I was the king of the behind-the-back pass on the court. I was an absolute assassin in wall-ball. I once punched a nigga in the back of his head so hard... Okay, maybe I'm not quite as proud of that one.

I got up and got behind her and grabbed my dick in one hand and her hips in the other. She squirmed and wriggled in anticipation. Taking my time, savoring the moment and my control, I gently rubbed the tip up and down her lips, basking in the juicy wetness within. She arched and flexed like a cat and moved back against me. I held off, though, for now I was in my element and I was gon make her appreciate this 11 inch. I rubbed down against her clit, hard and fat and throbbing to its own internal beat.

"You ready, mama?" I asked, voice low and deep and seductive.

"Yes, daddy," she sighed, arms outstretched, ass raised high, body totally submitted to my possession.

"Tell me you want it, baby," I said, sliding my dick down and forward to rest up and against her belly as the base of my shaft ground into her mound. She quivered and moaned.

"Ooo, I want it daddy."

"Tell me you like it, baby."

"Ooo, I like it daddy."

"Tell me you need, it baby."

"Ooo, fuck, daddy, I need it."

"Then tell me what you want, baby."

She looked back over her shoulder, looked back and up at me, looked at me with eyes I just realized I'd learned to see, filled with hopes and dreams I just now realized I wanted to help come to fruition, with a promise of a future that I just now realized I wanted to be a part of. She looked back and up at me and I felt truly and completely seen for the first time in my life, a sensation I will always carry and never forget. She looked back and up at me and said...

"Daddy, I want you to fuck the ever-loving shit out of me."

***

And now I'm fucking my homeboy's girl.

We have been here for literally four hours and I think this bitch plans to be here for four more. Which I'm totally cool with, because sweet pre-pubescent Jesus this bitch is amazing. I could do this all night. I could do this all day. Shit, how much vacation time I got cause I can do this all year. I can do this…

Wait, somebody's phone is ringing. Is it mine or hers? Look over and sure enough it's hers. And what that say on the ID…? Nah. Nigga nah. Hell nah. Not now. Son of a muthafuckin bitch. Of all times. Of all muthafuckin times.

THAT. MUTHA. FUCKIN. MIKE.

Public

"Oh, fuck! Oh, fuck! Oh, fuuuuuu... mmmphmmm."

That last was muffled by me shoving her draws into her mouth.

"Shorty, for the last time: SHUT. UP. You gon get us arrested out here!"

She looks back at me, eyes rolling into the back of her head, tears streaming down her cheeks, mouth gaped and stuffed with lace, and proceeds to throw it back even harder. Yup, much better.

It's bad enough that the sounds of what we're doing are unmistakable. My thighs are clapping her cheeks louder than the home side of a Warrior's game. Her pussy is so wet that it sounds like the test kitchen at the Kraft macaroni factory. And the grunts, groans and shrieks emanating from her throat sound like a nature special on the Discovery Channel, not of the mating habits of some noble African beast, but more like a pack of lions and hyenas tearing into a particularly fat and juicy wildebeest. If it wasn't so dangerous, it'd be epic.

As it is, I'm trying to keep this chick somewhere in the 6 range of the amplifier, because the group of kids and teenagers playing in the park on the other side of this fence haven't quite caught on yet.

Good Lord, what have I gotten myself into?

"Come on, baby; it's fun!" she'd said. "I've always wanted to do it outside," she'd said. "They call 'em like, voyeurs or voyeuristic or something," she'd said. The fact that she'd said this all while sucking my dick is why we're actually doing what she'd said.

And, Lord, the places we've done it.

The first time was the obligatory movie theater. No brainer, right? I mean, who doesn't fuck in a movie theater? Apparently, a lot of people. Especially prime time on a Saturday night. Especially when the movie you're watching is opening weekend of one of the highest grossing and attended movies in history. It's at that point I should've realized that this chick had some issues.

We'd made plans a few weeks before to catch the midnight showing of Avengers: Infinity War. I'm a big Marvel fan and was super geeked for what I knew was gonna be a spectacular installment. Her enthusiasm was as high as mine and I was excited; normally she only came along grudgingly, kinda like my trailing her to whatever romantic comedy she just "had" to see. So I'm hyped, telling her all about the plot lines I expect to culminate and emerge, what characters are likely to be featured, just what the final endgame will be, and she's just smiling along, asking me which sundress I think would be best. In hindsight, that should have been a clue. As should have been the fact that she deliberately disregarded underwear when she dressed in front of me, pointedly pointed out that she was not wearing any, and then grabbed and stuffed my hand into her crotch just to make sure I got the point.

I think I caught on.

We get to the theater to see the line wrapped practically around the building, and I'm almost disappointed. Almost, I say, because she'd been sucking my dick for the last 20 minutes and I was honestly damn-near too distracted to notice that we'd even pulled up. It wasn't until her lips pulled away from my knob that I resumed normal cognition. I let out a sigh of disgust because all the parking spots were way in the back.

"That's okay, daddy," she gon say, eyes twinkling, "I like it where it's dark."

Can you believe I actually missed that one? Yeah, I need to work on my read skills.

After circling forever, we finally find a decent spot, park and proceed to get in line. I'm standing behind her because this dress is hella short and hella flowy and she's got hella ass. Like ASS ass. Like, her ass got ass. I'm not saying it's the only reason I'm with

179

her, but — ass. As we were walking toward the line I could see a trail of eyes following her. I think I even heard a white boy shout. Who knew that Sir Mix-a-Lot was a ghetto prophet?

We take our place in the press of people and she backs into me, wrapping my arms around her tiny waist. It's actually one of my favorite positions to stand in. She's 5'2" and I'm 6'2", which makes her the perfect height for me to rest my chin comfortably on top of her head. Her hair is short and dreaded and always smells like coconuts and berries and shea butter and happiness, and I love just standing behind her and inhaling it. She's also incredibly petite — except for that ass; let us not forget that — and she fits amazingly in my arms. She's so warm and soft and delicate and pretty, basically a little golden angel.

An angel harboring a gaht damned sexual demon.

As we stand there, she softly and subtly grinds her ass into my dick.

180

"So you ready, daddy?" she asks, and I'm actually naive enough to think that she's talking about the movie.

"Oh, yeah," I reply, happily oblivious. "I've heard great reviews and the trailers have been awesome."

"Mmhmm," she hums, smiling and rubbing, giving me every possible hint that I am completely and categorically missing. And apparently, I'm the only one, because the people in the line around us seemed to know exactly what was up. I caught looks of surprise, admiration, and what looked suspiciously like pity from both the males and the females. They knew what I had yet to: this chick was on a mission, and all systems were about to be a big time go.

After what seems like an eternity, we finally get to the booth, purchase our tickets, rush to and through the concession line — why did she need so many damn napkins? — and make a beeline to our theater. Because it's opening night, they've got the movie showing on 12 screens, and because we didn't go for the 6D, air-cooled, super-shiatsu, Space Shuttle Challenger chairs, or the poly-panoramic, blow-out-your-retinas, cinescope-on-acid 3D "experience," we luck out and catch a theater that isn't packed to the gills. I look for my favorite seats: direct and absolute center. I know what they say about sound and viewing being optimized for any seat and location, but I take that with as much salt as my supposedly "lightly salted" popcorn. For me, if you're in the building, you need to be in the exact middle of the building or else you might as well be at home. And lo and behold, there were actually two spots free, right in the smack-dab center. I was shocked, surprised, elated, felt that the movie gods were smiling down upon me — and so you can imagine my shock, surprise, and deflation when she pulls me up and away.

"But, but, but..." I stammered, trying to slow her down. "Baby, the seats...and the middle...and the aisle..."

"I like it better up here, daddy," she said, dragging me into the no-man's land of the nosebleeds. Who in their right mind purposefully sits way up here? I mean, the lighting is way off, the sound gets that doppler effect, and there's almost always somebody doing something untoward in one of the corners.

Did I mention how bad I was at catching a point?

"It's okay, daddy," she said, turning and giving me a quick peck on the lips. "I'll make it up to you."

"Sure," I sigh in resignation, letting her pull me along. "I've the utmost confidence in that." What's that thing they say about "famous last words?"

We get to the top, find a dark, desolate corner, and settle into our seats. I sit back and, with some trepidation, stretch my frame into the unfamiliar space. To my surprise, it's actually quite comfortable. Come to find out, there's a little more legroom available in these upper rows. Who knew? Well, I console myself, I

183

might be out of prime viewing position, but at least there're a few perks. I smile to myself indulgently, lean over, and give her a quick peck on the forehead, forgiving her for what I'm graciously willing to write off as a minor inconvenience, and prepare to settle myself in for the adventure ahead. She smiles back, leans in, and snuggles against me, hands twining in mine, head resting prettily on my shoulder. It's a perfect, picturesque moment — that lasts all of 90 seconds before she slides her hand down my pants.

"Whoa!" I damn near shout, trying not to jump out of my seat and draw attention to us. "Baby, what are you doing?"

She looked at me like I was a simpleton, and I gotta admit I deserved it. *What are you doing?* I ask with her hand wrapped firmly around my dick. If I couldn't figure that out, I needed professional help.

"Playing with your dick," she said, rolling her eyes while massaging my meat. "Duh."

"Yes, I realize that," I stammered, trying to

184

maintain composure, cause shorty is really, REALLY good at that. "My question is *why* are you playing with my dick." She rolled her eyes again at my obvious stupidity.

"First, because it's actually MY dick." I actually couldn't disagree with her, there. Over the course of the time we'd been together, she'd laid absolute and final claim to it. I'd been with my fair share of females in my 22 short years, but nobody, and I mean absolutely nobody, could do with my dick the things this chick could. It was almost mythical.

She massaged and continued.

"Second, because I wanna try something."

"Try what?" I asked, the edges of suspicion finally nudging my awareness.

"You know, 'something,'" she said, placing an emphasis I still somehow missed.

"Something like...?" I asked, seeking clarification I shouldn't have needed. She leaned in, kissed me, and spoke directly against my lips.

"Something like fucking the dog-shit out of you until I squirt all over the back of this seat in front of us."

Yes, she actually said that. Those were her actual words. Cute, petite, angelic little something, talking like a whole grown ass nigga in these streets. For half a second I was tempted to call HER daddy.

Please don't tell anybody I said that.

I was stunned, shocked, flabbergasted — and hard enough to chip titanium. Something about her aggressiveness, confidence, complete lack of fucks to give was an amazing aphrodisiac. She wanted to try something new, crazy, and exciting and I was ready to try it with her.

Dumbass.

I sat back and tried to burrow deeper into the shadows of the corner as she discreetly pulled my dick out. It twitched like a python in her petite hands, vibrating and thumping as she stroked its length. I bit my lip as she leaned over and licked the tip.

186

"Mmm," she moaned, lapping at the head and smiling up at me. "I swear I love how good you taste."

"And I love that you love it, lil mama," I responded with what I was sure was my best deep and confident voice. I mean, damn, I'm still a man, still that nigga, still in control of my shit —even though I felt my butt clench more than a little bit when I felt the tip of my dick hit her tonsils.

"You gon cum for me, daddy?"

"What? Already?" I stammered, trying to pretend that the thought hadn't literally just crossed my mind. Seriously, this chick had a cheat code for my dick or something, because I swear she could get me up and off in record time. I aint never been a minute man, but shorty's lips had me counting seconds.

"I wanna taste it, daddy." For emphasis she gave the tip another lick and then sucked the head like a blowpop. I tightened my grip on the armrests and tried to control my breathing.

"But baby," I managed to exhale, "we aint

187

even got out the credits yet."

She smiled around my dick and then slipped a hand lower to fondle my balls. I shut my eyes and tried to name every actor in the entire Marvel franchise. Fuck RDJ; the real talent was right here.

"That," she said, "means we've got a whole 'nother three hours to play. And I," she said with a lick, "want," a slurp, "the whole," a squeeze, "three." And with that she took me all the way down her throat. I had to bite back a scream. The couple three rows ahead of us turned around and stared in confusion.

"Wasn't that an amazing trailer?" I stammered, trying to stay in my seat as her throat milked me like a damn hoover. "Jamie Foxx is one of my favorite actors and I hear that's gonna be a great vehicle for him."

The girl rolled her eyes at me and the guy gave me one of those, "Nigga, right" looks and then turned back to the screen. I smiled nervously and tried to extricate my dick — which she was still swallowing like an anaconda at a buffet — from her throat.

"Shorty, you gon get us caught and thrown out of here!" She smiled and stroked me, licking her lips in satisfaction.

"No we won't, baby. They've seen worse."

Worse? There's worse? Worse than a chick auditioning to be the next Pinky during a decidedly non-Pinky movie? This flick isn't rated R, let alone X. I don't know what her definition of "worse" is, but I'm pretty positive it doesn't exceed this. It'd be different, maybe, if we were watching Deadpool, but the Avengers? What would Cap say?

"Baby, I..." I began, trying to explain the finer points of this somewhat convoluted concept. She stopped me.

"Shhh," she said, actually reaching up and placing her finger on my lips. Did I just get shushed? I just got shushed. I'm a grown man, and I've just been shushed. Aw naw. I'm a lot of things, but I am NOT a nigga to be shushed. I fixed my mouth to tell her just that when she shushed me again.

189

"Shhh," she said again, her finger pressed firmly against my lips while the tip of my dick was pressed firmly against hers. "Baby, just let me finish, okay?"

I look back at this now and laugh at how she said this like I actually had a choice in the matter. Which I did not. She and my dick had achieved their own form of communication and I was just along for the ride.

She gripped the base of my shaft with one hand and squeezed it in rhythm with what her throat was doing to the rest of me. With her other hand, she cupped and kneaded my balls in a perfect counterpoint. If I'd had more presence of mind, I'd have probably described some correlation between her technique and that of a master musician, even chuckling at the obvious pun in her playing with my "organ." If, as I said, I'd had more presence of mind. As it was, my mind was preoccupied with trying to maintain consciousness as she brought me to the biggest nut I'd yet in my young life experienced. The fact that I had to bite back my reactions seemed to quadruple the effect, which sent my senses into hyperdrive. She apparently realized this and began to suck me HARDER, and I damn near blacked out. The world behind my eyes split and exploded. I saw stars die and galaxies born. For a second, I swore I saw Dr. Strange pass me and wave on his way into a different dimension.

I'm a nerd with ho tendencies. Sue me.

After staring into the dark depths of what my enlightened and awakened awareness had been telling me was the bottomless well of universal time, I opened my eyes to find that it was just the theater going dark before the movie started. *Okay, I'm thinking, slowly putting myself away. We've survived. Yes, she just sucked my soul out, and yes I feel weaker than a baby deer on painkillers, and yes I'm in a relationship with the gaht danged Beelzebub of Blowjobs, but we are okay. We are fine. The movie's starting, she's had her fill, and now we can focus. We're good.*

I was actually, literally, saying these reassuring affirmations to myself when she grabbed my hand and shoved it between her legs. Her pussy dripped against my fingers as she rubbed them against herself before forcing two between her lips. She moaned as her walls began to clench around me, covering my hand in her sticky lust.

The couple in front of us turned around again, a flicker of disgust crossing the girl's face and one of annoyance crossing his. His seemed to say, "Nigga, you see what you doing to me down here? This bitch is actually trying to watch the movie and you back there reminding me of all the pussy I AIN'T getting. Help a brother out!"

It's amazing how much we black men can pack into a look.

I shrugged apologetically, trying to offer an explanation, but apparently the surge in my shoulders translated its way to my hand, causing her to moan again as my fingers twitched inside her. Breathing heavily, she scooted forward in the seat so she could spread her legs wider. Pushing my fingers deeper into her sopping snatch, she proceeded to pull out a titty and begin to suck.

I damn near panicked, certain that we'd gone too far. I was positive that this was the exact moment the lights would flare on, a gang of ushers and cops would storm up the aisles, and I and my Azazel with an Ass would be heading to the clink.

"Baby," I whispered fiercely, trying to be quiet but urgent. "You can't do that. What if somebody sees?"

She looked at me and pouted, mouth still full of fat, firm nipple. With a sigh, she began to put it back into her dress. Suddenly she stopped and pulled my hand from her twat, bringing it to her lips. Licking one finger, she wiped the other over and across her breast, leaving the nipple shiny and slick in the dim

193

light. I groaned and felt my dick lurch like a big block with a misfire. I lowered my head and she sighed and gripped the back of my neck as I proceeded to lick her clean.

I sucked and licked her lick a lollypop. Lapping the expanse of her areola, I tasted and teased the tiny bumps there. She giggled as it tickled. I flicked my tongue against the tip of her nipple, then blew on it, making it stiffen with the sudden rush of cold. I then sucked it back into the warm hold of my mouth, causing her to sigh with pleasure, a sigh which turned to a gasp of ecstasy as I took it between my teeth. With perfect pressure and precision, I worked my grip, until with a shake and a shudder, she came, biting back her screams as I bit her into ecstasy. When she finished, she put one hand between her legs and then into my mouth, pulling me close so that we could both savor the strong, sweet taste.

She put her breast back into her dress and my hand back between her legs. She grinned at me as if this was all completely ordinary.

"That was fun, huh?"

"Yeah, 'fun,'" I managed, trying to hide the fact that my brain was screaming that this was anything but. On the outside I smiled while on the inside I tried to decide what, in a parallel hell, I had actually gotten myself into. We'd wandered far off the edges of the map, and here there be monsters. A really pretty monster, mind you; a monster with a monstrous amount of ass; but a monster, nonetheless.

"So you're good, now, huh?" I asked, trying, vainly, to extricate my fingers from her dripping center. "I got mine, you got yours, everybody's a winner. We can watch the movie now, right?" She looked at me and laughed as if I were simple.

"Baby, nobody said you couldn't watch the movie. I know how much you wanted to see it, and I wouldn't do that to you."

I sighed in relief. It was all just a misunderstanding, a freaky interlude, of sorts. Yeah,

195

she'd threatened several hours of shenanigans, but in the end, that was all it was: a threat. She'd gotten me off, I'd gotten her off, and now we could get back to what we actually came here for. Having worked all that out, I actually felt pretty good about things.

While I was thinking, she'd slipped my fingers from her lower lips and back between the ones above. I shuddered at the sounds of her slurping them clean, my dick growing stiff again in my lap, but I willed myself to ignore it. Playtime had been fun, but it was over. Now it was time to focus.

If naive was a super power, I'd probably have been in the movie instead of watching it.

With one final, satisfied, sigh, she tongued the last of her love from my fingertips. She leaned over and kissed me, swirling her tongue against my lips and into my mouth, giving me another taste of her thick, tangy sweetness.

"So you ready, daddy?" she whispered, pussy painted breath flowing into my lungs and dick.

"Um, yeah?" I responded, hoping desperately that she was talking about the movie.

"Good!" And so fast that I barely had time to register it, she undid my jeans, pulled my dick out, turned around, and sat full upon it. I was up and in her so fast, I swear both me and my dick got disoriented.

"B-baby," I stuttered, fighting both the shock of the situation and the shocks of sensation as her pussy began to pulse around me. "I thought we were gonna watch the movie!" She turned her head to look at me, that smile that always made my heart skip, curving her perfect lips.

"Baby, we ARE watching the movie. We just happen to be watching it while fucking." As if to prove her point, she suddenly clenched her kegels, squeezing the head of my dick way up in that tight, wet place I loved so much, and I found myself suddenly acknowledging her logic.

People underestimate the wisdom imbued in a good, wet pussy.

197

Her back to me, she began a slow and easy grind in my lap. I slid my hands under the hem of her dress, resting them on her thick, golden hips. Laying my head back, I sighed, enjoying the sensations as she moved on top of me. I was in perfect, heavenly bliss — right up until I remembered that I wasn't actually watching the movie. An explosion on-screen brought me to my senses.

"Oh, shit," I exclaimed, sitting up and forward. "What I miss? It sounded important." I tried to lean around her to see what was going on.

"I think the metal guy just did something to the green guy and the guy with the wavy hands, but I'm not sure."

I could've cried, partially for her complete inability to keep track of things as well as her complete lack of giving a damn. Also, partially, for just how good the shit was that she was doing to my dick.

"Baby, this is kind of important!" I grabbed her hips, trying to move her off of me so I could see what was going on. She stopped me, taking my hands and pulling them forward and in between her legs, pressing them against her slick mound.

"You're right, baby. I'm sorry. Here, let's try this. "

"Try this" meant leaning forward and placing her elbows on the back of the seat in front of us, giving her a better position from which she began to bounce on my dick, not quite the solution I had in mind. I tried to stop her, tried to push her off and away. (I'll admit that it was a pretty feeble attempt. What can I say? She's REALLY good at that.) However, she took my hands and forced them back between her legs, sliding them up and down her box as she slid up and down my dick. I was trapped, stuck, immobilized — and, heaven help me, loving the fuck out of it. She looked back over her shoulder and smiled.

"Now, isn't that better?" she asked, mid-gyration. "And look: you can see the movie!"

She was actually right. She'd leaned so far

forward that I COULD see the movie. Unfortunately, I could *also* see her ridiculously fat ass as it worked its ridiculously fat magic on me. That muthafucka was in serious motion, bouncing, swirling and grinding like it had a mind of its own. She looked back at me again and, with a smile, began to twerk it on me. I bit my lip and shut my eyes, trying to fight the rising panic of a rising nut.

She had no such reservations.

With some kind of carnal telepathy, she always seemed to know when I was close to going over. I felt movement and cracked my eyes to see her looking at me with an expression I knew only too well. Oh, hell...

"Baby," she whispered, voice husky with lust, eyes hooded with anticipation, breasts somehow back out of her dress and back in her hands. "You ready to cum for me?"

Considering that all my energy was currently being employed in an effort to prevent that very thing, I could only nod mutely and helplessly. She smiled, licked her lips and then her nipples, and swung into hyperdrive.

"Then cum with me, daddy."

It was that "with" that shot something special through my system, the idea of that synergy, that union, that final and beautiful harmony. I held a special place in my heart for the thought of two people being joined so completely and perfectly, so in tune with and in one another, that they shared everything, even the bounding glory of simultaneous climax. It was so beautiful it almost made me cry...

...is what I'd like to say I was thinking.

In reality, all that deep, beautiful, romantic shit was being overridden by the thought that I was gonna blow a hole through this bitch's cervix in T-minus 10...9...8...

She moaned as she felt me begin to fuck her back, driving up and into her to meet and match her thrusts. As my hands gripped her thick hips for purchase and speed, she reached between her legs to finger her clit and fondle my balls. The sounds of our activities were unmistakable, from the loud clappage of cheeks, to the wet slap of her pussy against my shaft. Fortunately, we were in one of the movies many climactic battle scenes — talk about timing, right? — and so were unnoticeable.

I suddenly felt her pussy clench tighter around me, a sign of what was coming. She picked up speed and motion, bouncing and gyrating with renewed ferocity. She was close and was driving me closer. I held onto her hips, squeezing and gripping and slapping as she fucked me into oblivion.

"Daddy," she moaned, surprising me. She could talk during this? I'd damn near lost the power of speech in the last few minutes.

"Y-yes?" I managed to stammer back.

"Daddy," she said again, moaning louder. I could see the profile of her face where it leaned against the seat before us. The lights played against her skin, casting it in shadow and then relief, an effect that was quite beautiful. It reminded me just how gorgeous this girl was, how pretty, how beautiful, how...

"Daddy," she moaned again, snapping me out of the moment and back into that snapper.

"Yes?" I squeezed out again, fighting the mounting pressure of her pussy pressing on my dick.

"Now, daddy." And with no further preamble, she came. And she was true to her word, because when she did, she squirted all over the seat in front of us. Actually, it was a few seats, the floor, my jeans, my J's... It was like sitting front row at a Shamu show.

It was all too much for me, and with a muffled scream, I shook and then exploded inside her. My dick shot off like a rocket, hitting her with a full blast like an Iron Man plasma cannon. Like Thor's hammer. Like Thanos' gauntlet. If you asked, Hulk had definitely SMASHED.

You get the idea.

We sat there, sucking air and sanity, fighting to

203

regain composure and decency. She'd taken my hands, which had been wrapped around her, and wrapped them around her breasts as she fought to catch her breath. My head was pressed against her back where I could feel her heartbeat pounding in time with my own. Our combined cum dripped down around my shaft, pooling against my base and balls. Several seconds passed before either of us could speak.

"That was good, huh?" she asked, smiling, kneading her breasts with my hands. *Good*, I thought. *Good? Bitch, that was INSANE.* I'd never had an experience like that and doubted that I ever would again. I managed to grunt out a noncommittal "yeah."

She slid back into her seat, smoothing her dress and putting her breasts away. We both looked down at my dick and laughed at its sorry, slick state.

"I guess now I know what all the napkins were for," I laughed, reaching for a handful. She laughed, too, but then stopped me, a mischievous twinkle in her eye.

"Or..." she said, before engulfing me between her lips. I threw my head back and exhaled, enjoying the rush as she licked and sucked me clean.

When she finished, she sat up and kissed me. I tasted both of us on her lips, a sensation not wholly unpleasant. I started to put my dick away, but she stopped me.

"Baby: the movie," I said gently, trying to extricate her hands.

"But it's just so pretty," she pouted, fingers soft and warm as she stroked the shaft. It began to stiffen as she worked her magic. I groaned, hard again in seconds.

Suddenly her eyes widened and she looked from it to me, a wicked, dangerous grin forming on her lips. I was instantly suspicious. Stroking me a little harder and faster, she leaned toward me and whispered.

"That *was* good, wasn't it, daddy?"

"It was great, baby," I responded, wondering, exactly, where this was headed. She continued.

"And I was just thinking of something else good we could do." As her fingers were wrapped around my head, fondling and stroking, I was finding it hard to concentrate.

"Oh?" I managed, slipping, again, toward a lust-laced stupor.

"Something I always wanted to try," she murmured into my ear as she licked my earlobe. I twitched in response.

"W-what's that?" I stuttered, afraid to ask but too caught up not to.

In answer, she let go of my dick, turned away from me and raised her dress, exposing that massive, monstrous, impeccable ass.

"I wanted to try it in my ass."

...

...

...

You ever hear somebody yell "Check, please!" in a movie theater?

I was done. Fuck this movie, fuck this theater, fuck Iron Man, fuck Captain America, fuck the entire gaht damn squad. Fuck Marvel in general and Stan Lee in particular. Y'all can have this shit. I'm out.

I grabbed her hand and we hit the nearest exit at a trot. The last thing I saw was the couple in front of us, the girl giving us the finger, the dude with a solitary Denzel tear in his eye. But I gave absolutely no fucks. I'll catch this shit on DVD. Cause right now I'm gonna go blow every last bit of this bitch's back out.

***

And that was three months ago. Since then, we've done it some of everywhere: department store dressing rooms, college conference rooms, a Costco parking lot. Two days ago it was in the Backstage at Macy's, the day before that, the state historical museum (don't even ask how we managed that). And now we're here, getting down next to a playground.

207

I'd feel bad if it didn't feel so damn good. And good, sweet, prepubescent Jesus, it feels so damned good. She's throwing it back like a semi with a hemi and, and I'm throwing it right back to her like demon with a diesel. This shit is epic, extraordinary, exemplary...

Annnd somebody's recording us.

And now other people are looking.

And that woman just called the cops.

sigh

Fuck.

Three's Company

Eric was sitting at his laptop doing code compiles when he heard his phone buzz. He took another glance at his work, making sure the lines were syncing, then picked it up.

"Hey boo," the text read, and he smiled and shook his head. Taniese. He chuckled at the affectation she used, both of them knowing that they were anything but "boos." He tapped the screen and typed back.

"Sup shorty?"

She immediately replied.

"Nothing. Wyd?" He smiled again as he glanced at the time. It was 12:40 am, and there were only so many reasons somebody would be asking that question at that time of night. And with Taniese, there was only one. He decided to play coy.

"Shit, nathan. Just sitting here working on this

new project."

The phone buzzed again immediately.

"Sooo that means you're busy?"

Eric laughed to himself, amused by this game they always played. Taniese was one of what he politely called his Kit Kats, which, in blunt speak, meant a chick he had in rotation when he needed to get broke off. They'd been kicking it for a few years now, and even though it was always awesome, he never felt tied down or committed to anything more or deeper. The fact that she didn't either was a definite plus. They were happy fuck buddies, emphasis on the fucking. He typed again.

"Actually kinda. Tryna get this new app up and off my plate so I can move to the next one."

The phone buzzed again.

"Awww, so that means you aint got time for me?" He could actually hear her pout, something he found as endearing as it was adorable even though he knew it was complete bullshit. Most of what Taniese said or did was not to be believed and never to be taken at face value, but once you understood that, she was surprisingly easy to work with. She wasn't "bad;" she just wasn't serious, and Eric found no complication with the distinction. It was just how she was, but unlike most females, she didn't try to hide it. They had their own system of language and interaction and it suited them just fine.

"I mean... Kinda depends on what you need," he texted back, smiling and waiting for the inevitable. He was not disappointed.

"I need that dick, duh."

He laughed to himself at her bold brazenness. One thing you could never say about Taniese was that she was shy. "Shy" had absolutely no space in her vocabulary.

Still playing it, out he responded.

"That is so sweet. However, I am kind of in the middle of something."

Three bubbles popped up in the window

211

letting him know that she was replying. When the message finally came through, he smiled and grabbed his dick. It was a shot of her laying back on her bed, completely naked, thighs spread, with two fingers buried in her already wet pussy. Another text came through.

"Sooo, you still busy, or nah?"

He laughed, already shutting his computer down. The pic was what they called the Bat Signal. Back and forth banter was cool, and on slower, more relaxed days, it was fine for a little foreplay action. But when one of them really wanted to get down, they'd send the other a pic. It was an unequivocal call to action — some serious fuck action. He stared at the pic and licked his lips, already anticipating licking hers.

"Suddenly, not so much."

"Good," she immediately replied, and then the three dots appeared again. What came through next surprised him. It was another picture, but this time of a completely different girl. This was a tall, thick-thighed yellow bone, posing nude in a selfie. His eyes were immediately drawn to the width of her hips, the full size and shape of her large tits — complete with nipple rings, his weakness — and one of the fattest pussies he'd ever seen, crowned by a thicket of curly red hair. "Damn," he muttered, sitting up. "This just got interesting."

Another text came through.

"You like?"

He almost felt like she could see him through the phone, sensing his reaction.

"Shit, you already know. One of yours?"

"New booty. Tried her out a few times and she go. Told her that I wanted sumn a little freakier tonight, though, and that I knew just the nigga for the job."

"Shit. Good looking," Eric replied in genuine appreciation.

"You know I got you, daddy. Lol." He could

actually hear her laugh. He liked her laugh. It was always free and honest and devoid of the general bullshit she could fall into when talking. He texted back.

"ETA?" He had to straighten a few things if he was about to have company.

"Gimme 15. I'ma scoop her and then we're on the way."

"Bet," he replied, already anticipating what was about to go down.

"Door open?" She sent this with an emoji of a key.

"You already know." He paused and then continued. "You sure she can go?"

He could see her smirk even as she typed.

"Have I let you down yet?"

He had to admit that she hadn't. For all her difficult and far too often childish ways, one thing Taniese was was an excellent judge of female ability. Not a lot of chicks could take what he could give, but she seemed to know just who could. It was an amazing talent, and one of the things, ironically, that he genuinely respected about her.

"You right. Word. Y'all get in motion, then. I'll be here."

"See you soon, daddy," came the reply, and Eric rubbed his hands in eager anticipation.

***

Exactly 15 minutes later his front door opened, admitting the two women. He was in the kitchen, pulling a bottle of wine out of the chiller, so didn't see them as they entered. When he finally turned, he had to give Taniese another nod of respect. This chick she had brought with her was bad. He'd already seen her naked, true, but there are some women who seem to get sexier when clothed. As a consequence, it made getting them naked again seem like unwrapping a Christmas present.

Taniese was wearing a short sundress which he

215

was sure she was naked underneath; she knew he liked easy and ready access so always came prepared. Her friend, though, was wearing a black spaghetti strap midriff shirt and a pair of black tights. And them mufuckas was TIGHT. He had to stop himself from staring as she walked further into the room. Her thighs were damn near as thick as his, and he was a big dude. Standing 6'4" and 240, he was what they called linebacker built. He'd actually played football in college but didn't have the interest or, were he being honest, the aptitude to go further, so just focused on his studies instead. He figured that since the school was paying, he was gonna make them give him their money's worth. He'd settled into computers and had been doing well for himself since. He never lacked for friends or women, though he never really had time for either. He liked a constant rotation of company, something that suited his quick-firing mind and free-flowing lifestyle. Thus Taniese. And thus this stallion she was with.

The former walked up to him and gave him a hug — and then immediately stuck her tongue down his throat and her hand down his shorts.

"Mmm," she purred, gripping and caressing his dick. "Hey baby. And hey you, too," she laughed, addressing *him* this time. She and his dick had their own special greeting. She kissed him again as he slipped his hand under the hem of her dress and cupped her ample ass, confirming that, yes, she'd come down for the get down.

"Hey lil mama," he smiled, enjoying the feel of her hands on him. "How you been?"

"Oh, you know," she said leaning back and stretching languidly. "Good as always."

He laughed because they both knew that "good" was a rather broad term when it came to her.

"I bet." He slapped her playfully on the ass and watched it bounce in response. Inclining his head toward the other girl, he eyed her up and down. "So, you gonna introduce me," he asked, "or is this gonna be a spectator sport?"

She turned to her friend who was openly returning his gaze, a look of appreciation in her eyes and the hint of a challenge on her lips.

"This," Taniese said turning," is Joy. Joy, meet E."

Eric extended his hand, which she took. He noticed her perfectly manicured nails and the warmth and softness of her grip.

"A pleasure, lady."

"You promise?" she said, and then laughed at the look on his face. "Oh, I hope you didn't think I was the shy type."

"Shit, not anymore." And with that he caught her by the waist, pulled her into him, and grabbed two handfuls of her ass. She moaned as he palmed it, getting a feel for its solidity, heft and weight. Yeah, shorty was definitely sitting on something spectacular.

Good Lawd, he thought. *I might just hurt*

myself tonight.

His hands gripped and kneaded her ridiculously large and soft ass, pulling her up and against him. She pressed in to kiss him, their tongues passionately exploring each other. She ground against him, pressing her mound into his dick, gliding up and down its length. She definitely knew what she was doing and was down to do. Eric silently exulted, knowing that he was about to have an EXCELLENT evening.

Joy stepped back, pulled away by Taniese whose arms had come up to wrap around her, fondling her breasts. When she pulled her shirt up and off, Eric bit his lip. He almost didn't think it possible, but her tits were even better than they'd looked in the picture. At least DD's, they sat full and high, dark, perfectly round nipples against smooth yellow flesh, two pink studs peeking from each one. He licked his lips and then dipped his head to suck her nipples into his mouth as Taniese held them up and out to him.

Joy arched her back and moaned and then again louder as one of Taniese's hands slipped down the front of her tights. The combination of sensation and visual became too much.

"Okay, time to fuck," Eric announced straightening up. "You bitches not finna have me leaking all over my clean floor." They laughed as he led them back to the den and the couch therein.

Once there, Taniese pushed Joy back onto the soft leather cushions and began sucking her nipples. Joy's hands twined in Taniese's hair as she arched her back and closed her eyes. Meanwhile, Eric had kneeled behind Taniese and raised her dress. He groaned when he saw her spread there before him. Taniese had an ass like a watermelon and a pussy as fat as a plum. He often said that she was his favorite form of daily fruit intake. He knelt behind her and slid his tongue up the length of her lips. It was already extremely wet and sticky and sweet as a nectarine. She sighed and arched her back further, spreading her knees for him. He took his cue and turned over, letting her settle down into his face. Eric had a serious oral fixation, i.e. he absolutely LOVED to eat pussy. It was one of the things Taniese said she liked about him. The other, of course, was his dick.

Eric licked and sucked as Taniese ground into his face. She was one of the few women he knew that could ride his face and his dick with equal facility. She bounced her pussy against his lips as his hands palmed her ass. Back and forth, up and down, around and in circles, she fed him a steady diet of her thick juicy wetness. His dick jumped and thumped in rhythm to her movements.

Finally she sat straight up, grabbing his wrists and arching her back. She shuddered as she came, flooding his mouth. She gasped and shook as he ate her through her orgasm, cumming again in seconds. She said she'd never had multiples before him, didn't even believe it was possible. But Eric was a different breed, and he'd taught her a great many things during their sessions together.

Eventually she pushed herself off of him and lay to the side, one hand to her chest, the other between her legs as she tried to catch her breath.

"Fuck, I needed that," she said dreamily from her position on the floor.

"You know I always got you, shorty. It's what I'm here for." They both laughed at what was obviously a regular routine.

"Damn, I think I'm jealous." Joy had been watching as Taniese came, intrigue and lust mingling in her gaze.

"You just think?" Eric asked, eyebrow raised, eyes roving over her body.

"I KNOW I am — unless it's my turn." He was about to respond, but before he could, she'd grabbed him, pulled him close, and began to lick Taniese's cum off his lips. The sheer sexiness of it kicked his heart rate up a notch, and he tongued her back fiercely, biting and sucking at her lips as she opened herself to him. Her ass ground in circles on the couch as his hands massaged her back and breasts and nipples, their tongues clashing and collapsing together.

He broke away to catch his breath. His eyes slid over her body as her breasts rose and fell with her own heaving breaths. Gently, he placed one hand between her breasts and pushed her back onto the couch. She fell willingly, looking up at him, eyes hooded with lust and anticipation as he grabbed the waistband of her tights and began to pull them down. She raised herself to assist and then gasped at the sudden shock of his lips and tongue on her pussy. He hadn't even waited to pull her tights completely off; he left them wrapped around her legs, now pointed up and into the air. It was go time and he wasn't trying to wait.

"Oh, shit," she panted, gripping the couch to steady herself as he went to work. His hands wrapped around the meat of her thighs, pushing her legs further back to expose the fat, wet peach between. His

223

tongue dipped in and around, licking and sucking and virtually fucking her with its skill and intensity. Within seconds she was shaking and trying to push him away, an action that only told him to go faster. A moment later she stifled a scream as a stream of cum arced into the air.

"Oh, we got a squirter!" Eric leaned back and laughed as Joy shook and shuddered beneath him.

"Shit, even I didn't know that," Taniese replied in grudging admiration. She'd been watching the show, one hand on her nipples, the other buried between her legs, keeping herself entertained and ready while they played.

"Oh, you hadn't accomplished that yet?" Eric smirked as he bent down to lick Joy's slick, cum-drenched lips.

"Fuck you, nigga. You always tryna outdo somebody." She punched him playfully in the arm with one hand, continuing to finger herself with the other.

"Can I help it that I'm great?" he replied with

mock humility.

"Yeah, yeah, nigga, whatever. You just lucky I aint got a dick or I'd show your ass up."

"Actually, how bout you toot that ass up while you take this dick so we can get this shit started?"

"Daddy, you aint said nothing but a word." She hopped up, pulled her dress over her head, and slid into the space between he and Joy. She backed into him, spreading her legs and arching her back. In one smooth motion his shorts were down and off and his dick was poised at her entrance. Teasing her slit with its head, he called down to her.

"You ready, lil baby?" he asked, rubbing himself up and down the slow stickiness of her lips. In answer she rocked back, forcing him up and into her.

"You already know, daddy." She moaned as her pussy took and gripped him, causing them both to shudder.

"Then let's get this muthafucka started." And with that he went to work.

225

Grabbing her tiny waist above the flare of her hips, he set a hard, fast rhythm. With most chicks, he often had to ease into action, they not always being prepared for the length and girth of his dick. Most had to adjust slowly before they could take his full stroke. But Taniese was a rider and a G. She could take what he gave and give some back. They'd had some amazing sessions, fucking each other in ways that would've crippled lesser people.

As he pounded her pussy, she tongued her friend's. Lips wrapped around Joy's, she sucked and suckled her with panting abandon. Joy, for her part, was obviously appreciative. Eyes closed, back arched, she pulled and played with her nipples as she moaned in ecstasy.

"She pretty good at that, lil mama?" Eric asked her, chuckling while stroking. He put himself on autopilot, a trained ability that let him fuck and focus at the same time. In this way, he was able to give enjoyment while enjoying the show.

226

Joy's eyes cracked open and she smiled, eyes glazed with lust and satisfaction.

"Yeah, daddy. Lil baby got me and this pussy feeling *good* good." Eric felt the spasm of Taniese's laughter along his dick milliseconds before he heard it. She turned toward him, face slick and shiny with Joy's juices. She cocked an eye and smirked.

"Told you, my nigga. You always tryna outdo somebody, but sometimes you just accept that I'm great." Eric laughed at the return of his joke. He smacked her ass in response and punishment, but the sight of it jiggling and undulating beneath him caused his dick to jump, momentarily stuttering his stroke. Taniese felt it and laughed again.

"You good back there, my guy? You ain't getting caught up in this pussy, is you?"

"I'll show yo' ass 'caught up,'" he called back. Renewing his grip on her hips, he began to increase his speed, force and depth. This new gear kicked the pressure up a notch, resulting in turning Taniese into a veritable piston. Caught between the driving force of his dick and the yielding pressure of the pussy in her face, there was only one place for her to go, and she went gladly. Grunting and groaning with passion, she threw her ass back wildly, Eric catching and meeting her thrusts, chuckling at the sounds she made at each stroke.

"So what's that you were saying about getting caught up?" Eric asked from above her, hands wrapped around her waist, giving her nowhere to run as he fucked her into submission.

Taniese's response was muffled by Joy's thighs which had held a firm grip around her head ever since Eric's renewed stroke had sent a shock through her that sent her tongue up and deep into Joy's pussy. Joy instantly shuddered and shook, her limbs seizing up, locking Taniese against her. Joy found herself wondering, through the fog of sheer lust and pleasure wrapping her mind, if this nigga had somehow managed to fuck her THROUGH another bitch.

Taniese was used to this reaction; he'd done it to most of the chicks they'd shared. The first time, the experience was so unexpected, so new, so extreme, that both she and the other girl had run, scooting up, off and away. He'd laughed at them, perched on either end of the couch, panting and fanning themselves, stomachs and thighs quivering from the aftershocking sensations. He'd had to coax them back slowly, promising to be more gentle next time. But of course he wasn't. Women don't seem to realize it, but running from a dude during sex is like running from a dog: it's the fuck equivalent of "sic 'em." For the rest of that evening, he'd fucked both his partners into complete and utter submission. It was an experience Taniese often and fondly recalled — and one which she hoped would play out again tonight. In truth, it had already begun.

Between the pounding of Eric's dick and the pulsing of Joy's pussy, Taniese was being pushed up and over her threshold. She reached up and spasmodically grabbed Joy's breasts, hands overflowing with the soft, golden flesh, fingers tweaking the hard, ring-studded nipples. Both girls moaned as fresh streams of juice flowed, Joy's on Taniese's tongue, Taniese's down the length of Eric's dick. Their moans mingled with the clapping of Taniese's ass against Eric's thighs. Seeing their reactions and intuitively responding, he shifted into yet another gear, picking up speed and force until, with one final stroke, he slammed both of them into wild and screaming orgasm.

Shuddering and panting, both women collapsed, fighting to regain their breath and composure. Taniese, head resting against Joy's now spread and shimmering thighs, pulled off and away from Eric's dick. She wiped a lock of hair from her forehead then sat back, fanning herself. She ran her hands down her sweat-slick breasts and stomach before settling them between her legs. Rubbing herself low and slow, she turned lazy, hooded eyes on

Eric.

"My nigga, THAT is how you a fuck a bitch."

Eric laughed at her bluntness. Most of the time Eric didn't care for women that talked that way. He liked his women classy, not coarse or crude. But that was most of the time. It was different when smashing was involved. After all, all is fair in love and fucking.

"So you admit I'm that nigga?" he said, smirking and stroking his dick. Taniese noticed that it was still hard: long, strong, and covered in a slick sheen. She knew that was hers, a trophy well-earned — but one she wasn't going to give him the satisfaction of acknowledging.

"I mean, I aint say all that."

"Oh, is that doubt I hear?"

Taniese saw him moving toward her and threw up her hands, scooting away.

"Oh, no nigga; don't point that thing at me. A bitch needs a breather." Eric laughed then leaned down to kiss her. Their tongues mingled and danced

231

as his fingers played across her flesh: the taut buds of her nipples, the soft skin of her stomach, the hot and moist press between her legs. In moments she was breathing hard again, but pushed him off, laughing.

"Nigga, stop! You tryna kill a bitch in here!"

"Lightweight." He laughed and reached out to pinch her nipple.

"Lightweight my ass," she huffed, slapping his hand away. "Besides, you got a whole other pussy right there."

Eric cocked his head at Joy who still lay on the couch, seemingly oblivious to their exchange, her eyes closed, lips slightly parted, lost in her own little blissful world.

"You do have a point," he smiled, moving to position himself between her legs.

Joy had been quietly laying there, one hand lazily kneading her breasts, the other sliding fingers up, down, and between her nether lips. Her eyes snapped open when she felt Eric's tongue join them.

232

"Wake up, lil mama," he teased, nipping the hard little bud of her clit. "It's way too early to be tapping out." She moaned at the sensation, then used her fingers to open herself to him.

"Who said anything about tapping out?" Her breath caught as his tongue swirled around her, causing her pussy lips to plump and emit a fresh trickle of juice. She spread her legs, inviting him in further. "I was just waiting my turn."

"Oh, we got a real one, here!" Eric exclaimed, laughing. He slid his hands under her thighs, grabbing her ass and pulling her toward him. In return, she grabbed his dick and stroked it, rubbing it up and down against and between her lips. Eric grinned down at her, enjoying the view of her teasing herself. She smiled back, a challenge dancing across her full lips.

"Oh, you aint know, lil daddy? I'm real as a thousand dollar bill and twice as hard to come by."

"Is that right?" Eric replied, smiling and feeling himself stiffen in response.

"You already know," and she slid forward and against him so that the head of his dick parted her lips and slipped inside her. With a satisfied sigh, she began to grab her tits, cupping and squeezing them. Eric slowly worked himself into her, acclimating himself to her warmth and grip. His eyes slid up her body and met hers. They shone with lust and confidence. Joy licked her lips while wiggling her hips against him. "So is we gon fuck or talk," she teased, impatient. "'Cause I didn't really come here for conversation."

Taniese burst into gales of laughter from the floor beside them.

"I told you this bitch was legit, E!"

"Shit, I see. And I appreciate it." He leaned toward her. "High five, my guy!" Joy laughed as Eric and Taniese actually did it. In an instant, her laugh became a gasp as Eric shoved himself into her in one long, strong stroke. She arched her back and moaned as she felt his dick probing her depths, filling her to her core.

Eric ran his hands across her skin. It had blushed from golden to a rosy glow as if her whole body was on fire with trapped heat and passion. He watched the smooth muscles of her stomach flex and contract against his strokes, he imagining and she feeling him poking at the back of her belly button. Her ass overflowed his hands, her thick thighs shaking and trembling against him. He loved how she cupped and fondled her breasts, and caught himself groaning as she pulled one of the ring-studded nipples into her mouth. She moaned when she felt his lips and tongue on the other. Grabbing the back of his head, she pulled him to her, staring into his eyes as their tongues danced and mingled together across the shared erect, brown bud. The look of sheer, radiating lust and passion in her eyes threatened to push him too far. With a shudder and a chuckle, he sat up, renewing his grip on her hips, and set himself to a more sedate pace inside her.

"I say, damn, lil mama," he laughed, rocking

and rotating within her, "you tryna get a nigga in trouble."

Joy smirked, looking at him over her breasts as she licked and sucked and bit each one. She laughed at his reaction, the way he bit his lip and shook his head while he tried to focus against the twitching of his dick inside her.

"Oh, was you gon cum for me already, lil daddy? You aint gotta be shy."

Eric laughed loud and full, his dick jumping and thumping against her walls. The sensation pushed her close to her own edge and she bit her lip in anticipation.

"Shy? Nah, never that."

"Oh, so you scared then?" Joy smiled as her words had their desired effect. Eric, taking this as a challenge, had increased the speed and force of his thrusts inside her. Her pussy tightened in response.

"Scared of what, pray tell?" he asked her, shifting his position slightly to introduce a new angle to his stroke. They both exhaled as he found a new, tighter spot.

"Scared a bitch gon turn yo ass out," she replied around her rapid breath and building ecstasy. He was fucking her toward her third orgasm of the night, and it promised to be the biggest yet.

Eric grunted, placed her legs up and onto his shoulders, and leaned forward, pushing himself in even deeper. He bit her calves, eliciting an exclamation of shock and pleasure. He could feel his dick growing thicker and harder as his orgasm built within him.

"Who turning who out in this muthafucka? Your girl should've told you about me: I turn mo chicks than a carousel."

"My dude, that was corny af." Taniese laughed as she got up from where she'd been lying on the floor. She smacked his ass, eyeing the taut flex of his muscles as they bunched and relaxed with the rhythm of his thrusts. "I'ma need you to retract that," she said, climbing up onto the couch. Eric knew what was coming next. In one smooth motion, she threw her leg over Joy's face and sank down, lowering her pussy into the other girls lips. Joy started in surprise and then moaned with desire, reaching up and around to grasp Taniese's hips, pulling the girl deeper into her mouth. Taniese sighed as Joy's tongue went to work. Eric leaned forward to lick the line between Taniese's shoulder blades, then pushed Joy's legs even further up and apart. These were championship rounds, and he was going for the belt.

"You right," he replied, already increasing pace. "That wasn't my best moment."

"Pussy got you discombobulated, huh?" Both girls laughed, Joy into the wet, warm confines of Taniese's peach.

"Oh, so everybody got jokes today? I'ma show yo ass 'discombobulated,'" and as before, he shifted into a higher gear.

Joy moaned and squirmed as his dick pounded

her relentlessly, filling her deeper and harder with every thrust. Her pussy creamed around him, gripping and gliding against him. She felt him in her womb, her stomach, her chest. The torment of her orgasm was building in pulsing waves, crashing toward a mind-bending climax.

Taniese squirmed atop Joy's face, gyrating and grinding down and into her mouth. Joy's tongue alternated between flicking Taniese's clit and probing deep inside her. Her hands gripped her ass for what seemed like dear life, pulling her against her, feasting on Taniese's pussy as her own pussy feasted on Eric's dick. Taniese was filled and thrilled by their synergy — and then squealed when she felt Eric grab her hair, pulling her into a soul-shattering arch.

Eric felt himself going over. The sight, sound, smell of good, wet pussy — the sheer sensation was too much. His impending orgasm boiled inside his balls, heavy and hot. The muscles at the base of his shaft twitched and tightened, preparing for the beautiful purge of release. Every nerve on every millimeter of his dick was alive and on fire. This was gonna be epic.

With a gasp and a soul-grinding groan, Taniese came, flooding Joy's mouth with her cum. The sudden rush of taste and sensation set Joy off, and *she* came, squirting in shiny crystal jets against Eric's stomach and chest. Eric's eyes almost rolled into the back of his head as he rushed to pull himself from her. With a groan and a shudder, he grabbed his dick and came all over the two girls. Jet after jet after jet after jet exploded from his tip, cascading over them, falling in glistening strands onto Joy's hips and stomach and breasts, and Taniese's ass and back. The combined sheen of their sweat and sex made their bodies shine like ebony and mahogany and marble statues in the light. It was a work of art — the art of good fucking.

Eric collapsed back onto his heels, drained and, for the moment, spent. He rolled his neck and shoulders, feeling their sweet ache, tight from the

240

aftershocks. He watched as Taniese slowly crawled off of Joy's face, standing to work the kinks out of her own frame. Joy lay still, panting slightly, her stomach quivering with her attempts to gather air and sanity. She'd cum so hard that she'd thought for a second that she would black out. She had to make a note not to tempt this nigga too much, because he could back up everything he said and then some.

Taniese wandered into the bathroom and returned with a warm towel which she used, first, to clean Eric, then turned so that he could clean himself from her back and ass. He was about to do the same for Joy, but Taniese waved him off. He smiled, knowing where this was heading. Leaning over the prone girl, Taniese went to work. Instead of using the towel, she used her tongue, lapping the thick, creamy strands of Eric's cum from Joy's warm skin. Joy stretched and purred like a cat as Taniese licked her clean. When Taniese's tongue slipped along her hips, Joy sighed with pleasure. When her tongue dipped

241

into her navel, she tensed and tingled at the tickling touch. And when Taniese's warm, soft lips wrapped and swirled around her nipples, licking up the thick pools of cum that had gathered there, she moaned and slid her fingers into herself.

Eric watched, one eyebrow raised in appreciation. He slowly stroked his dick, already heavy and growing harder in his hands. He was definitely ready to start another round. Feigning annoyance, he broke the reverie.

"So y'all just gon forget I'm over here, huh." Taniese cut her eyes at him, her lips and tongue still wrapped around Joy's nipple.

"What you mean? We was literally just fucking, like all of two minutes ago."

"Yeah, but a lot can happen in two minutes." For emphasis, he stood, his dick hard again, swinging long and slow in the air. Joy, who'd been watching Taniese work over her breasts, now shifted her eyes to Eric and they widened in surprise.

"Damn, you for real ready to go again already?"

Eric laughed as he held himself, slowly stroking it as they watched.

"Taniese didn't tell you about me, huh?"

"Bitch," Joy scolded, half in frustration, half in awe. "You did not tell me this nigga was the Energizer Bunny." Taniese laughed, pulling away from Joy's breasts. She lay back against the couch and began to play with herself, eyes on Eric's engorged dick.

"Yup, this nigga can GO go. It's one of the main reasons I fuck with him. When a bitch need to get for real broke off, he's a guaranteed bet."

"Damn," Joy murmured, eyes still locked on Eric's swaying member. "I might have to put myself on the team, then." Taniese and Eric laughed at the seriousness of her pronouncement.

"Aye, you def getting off on the right foot. Your application is solid and respectable. However..."

"However, what?" she asked, suspiciously. A

wicked grin lit Eric's face as he continued.

"However, before I add you to the crew, I gotta see what that mouth do."

Joy immediately felt herself start to get wet again. Eric's dick was long and dark and thick and she'd been waiting to taste it all night. She sat up from the couch and reached out to him. Smiling, he stepped forward and put himself in her outstretched hands. With a lick of her lips and a soft moan, she slid him into her mouth.

Eric sighed, his head falling back as the sensation rippled through his body.

"Damn, lil mama," he said, hands coming to rest on the back of her head. "You off to a damn good start."

"Is that right, daddy?" she asked around the tip of his dick. She was sucking him with the precision of practice and pure personal pleasure. Her tongue alternated between swirling around his head and lapping along his shaft, never losing its grip or force.

With one hand she cupped and kneaded his sac, juggling its full and heavy weight. With the other she stroked him methodically and rhythmically, milking out streams of pre cum. He let out a moan when he felt his tip hit her tonsils.

"Ya'll making that look mighty good over there," Taniese called out, her voice edged with equal parts appreciation and lust.

"Shit, it's getting mighty good over here," Eric laughed, guiding his meat in and between Joy's lips.

"Well, hell, y'all mind if a bitch get in on the action?"

"Aye, you know me: the more the merrier." They all laughed, Joy's coming out from around the tip of Eric's dick lodged firmly at the back of her throat.

Taniese dropped to her knees on the floor beside Joy and rubbed her hands together like a kid waiting for candy.

"Hey, E: do that thing you do." From the

corner of her eye, Joy saw her grinning and bouncing like she was about to win a prize.

"You mean the..."

From her vantage, Joy saw him make a strange movement with his hands.

"Yup, that's the one," Taniese replied, eyes full of mischief and excitement.

Joy was about to ask them what the hell they were talking about when she felt Eric lean forward, grab her waist, hoist her into the air, and then *flip her over*. She found herself hanging upside down, her thighs wrapped around his head while her lips remained wrapped around his dick. She didn't get enough time to register her surprise before she felt Eric's lips wrap around her pussy. When Taniese scooted between Eric's legs and took his balls into her mouth, Joy couldn't help herself. Pulling her mouth off of Eric's dick, she laughed at the craziness of it all.

"Ya'll muthafuccas really on some Fuck du Soleil shit, huh?"

Taniese laughed and kissed the still glistening tip of Eric's dick.

"Told you fucking with us wasn't no game."

"Shit, you wasn't EVEN lying. I aint never done no shit like this, but I fa sho wanna do it some more."

"Lemme see what my schedule is looking like Thursday." Eric laughed, sticking his tongue back between her upturned lips.

"I was already plotting on Thursday," Taniese said, tongue flicking the underside of his nuts.

"Well my schedule just got completely free!" Joy laughed and slid her mouth back down and around Eric's dick.

Waist wrapped in his strong, steady arms, Joy rode Eric's face while she let his tip ride her tongue. Her hips ground in circles and dips as she twerked against his face. Eric watched with mounting passion as her fat, yellow ass undulated and bounced and shook. Each ripple of her hips corresponded to an equal one in his dick, and the feeling was

247

extraordinary.

For her part, Joy was loving every second of it. The sounds of Eric slurping on her pussy while she and Taniese slurped his dick drove her crazy. She normally kept her eyes closed while giving head, preferring to be in her own little world of pleasure, but now she kept them open so she could watch Taniese work below her. Joy had never seen anybody suck a man's sac that way. Taniese didn't just lick or peck at it; she gave it her full and lustful attention. Joy could tell by the slight tremoring in Eric's legs that it was working. But more than the technique, Joy was turned on by how much Taniese apparently enjoyed it. She moaned and slurped around his nuts, one hand deep between her legs, rubbing and fingering her pussy. At one point, Taniese caught her looking at her and pulled away. Sensing a cue, Joy pulled her lips from Eric's tip and the two shared a deep, wet, passionate kiss, sucking each other's tongues and lips as hungrily as they'd just been sucking his dick. When Joy took Eric back into her mouth, and Taniese resumed her place on his nuts, they maintained eye contact, an unspoken challenge sparking the air between them.

Eric knew something was up when he felt the girls' grip and rhythm increase. His arms tightened around Joy as he fought to maintain control and balance. His tongue drove even deeper into her pussy and was rewarded with fresh waves of sweet cream. From the quickening pace of Joys' bouncing hips, and the increased volume of moans, he could tell that both girls were close to another climax. Within seconds they both exploded, screaming wetly around his shaft and sac. He felt himself on the edge, and…

Joy suddenly felt herself being pitched off and onto the couch. Orienting herself, she heard Taniese laugh as Eric stumbled off and away.

"What's the matter, lil daddy?" Taniese teased him as she watched him try to hide the wobble in his legs. "Little more than you can handle?"

"Man, y'all tryna set a nigga up in here. Tryna

have me turn in my man card." Eric was a comical sight, pacing back and forth and shaking his head, his dick still hard and bouncing in rhythm before him. "Y'all aint finna turn ME into the bitch in here."

"It's okay, lil daddy," Taniese laughed. "We won't tell nobody."

"You know damn well I don't trust you. You gon be all over Twitter and IG talking shit. Nope, not bout me you won't. Not today."

"Aw, come on back, E," Joy said, joining in. "We aint gon hurt you — too much."

Eric cast them a disgusted look and both girls laughed at him again.

"Man, fuck y'all." He turned and started for the kitchen. "I'm finna grab a Gatorade; anybody want anything?"

"Nah, I'm good," Taniese said from where she lay stretched out on the floor. She smiled and stroked herself, relaxing as the last ebbs of her orgasm radiated through her.

"I'm straight, too," Joy added, from her perch on the couch. She looked down at Taniese, running her eyes across her curves and glistening caramel skin. They slid over her full, round breasts with their hard, dark nipples, and came to rest on the plump wet nest between her legs. Taniese caught her looking and laughed.

"You 'straight,' bitch, huh?"

"Bitch, whatever," Joy replied, cutting her eyes. "You know what I meant."

"Oh, yeah?" Taniese teased her. "Why don't you come down here and show me."

Moments later, Eric walked back into the room and shook his head. He cast a quick glance to the ceiling and uttered a quiet "Thank You."

Joy's fat, round, yellow ass was in the air, bouncing in time against Taniese's lips. Eric watched as the darker girl lapped and suckled the fat peach above her, swirling her tongue over, around, and inside it. He could hear Joy returning the favor, her

251

face buried between Taniese's thighs, sucking and fucking her with abandon. Eric felt his dick throb as he watched and had a sudden, perfect idea.

Kneeling down behind them, he kissed Taniese on her forehead which caused her to tilt toward him. He slid his tongue against her lips and into her mouth, tasting Joy's musky sweetness.

"That's some good shit," he murmured against her lips.

"For real, for real," she smiled back at him.

"You tryna share," he asked, sliding his tongue into her mouth again.

"You already know, lil daddy."

Joy was oblivious to their conversation — until she felt the sudden thrill of two pairs of lips: one on her clit and the other on the lips of her pussy. She was just adjusting to the sensation when she suddenly felt both lips replaced by tongues, sending her up and over the edge.

Eric and Taniese licked and sucked her through

two rapid-fire orgasms, her body convulsing in waves and spasms. She thought she'd reached her peak, that she could go no higher, until she felt Eric's tongue slide into her ass. The shock made her scream as she squirted full into Taniese's mouth, the flow thick and sweet like ripe nectar. She came and came again, each one stronger than the one before.

Finally, she was ready to tap out. She knew they'd tease her for it, knew that they'd laugh and joke, but she didn't care. She'd been sent to her furthest and sexiest limits, and she was well and completely spent. This was the best sex she'd ever had in her life, and she was ready to lay back and savor it.

She was preparing to pull herself away, ready to take a breather and possibly a nap. She figured that after such an intense experience, they had to be, too. A little rest, a little drank, and they'd call it a night. That's what she was thinking — right up until she felt Eric slam his dick into her, sending her off into another soul-shaking orgasm. Hands locked on her hips, gripping and guiding her, he fucked her unmercifully while Taniese sucked and suckled her clit from below. She found herself trapped between them, locked in their rhythm, shaking and screaming as she came over and over and over again, more than she'd ever had before, more than she'd ever thought possible. If this was what REAL fucking was, she thought, sign her the fuck up.

Eric felt himself thicken and throb inside the tight hold of Joy's walls. Having held back earlier, he knew that this was going to be a much bigger affair. As if by some hormonal signal, Taniese sensed his impending release and started rushing toward her own. Throwing up her legs, she wrapped them around Joy's head, pulling her deeper into her wet and throbbing mound. Joy sucked her feverishly, using the shocks of her own orgasms as fuel to push Taniese to her own.

Suddenly, Taniese stiffened and screamed, her

climax ripping through her in a monumental wave. Not even knowing she was capable, she squirted, showering Joy's face and lips with a glistening torrent of her cum. Joy lapped and slurped it greedily, somehow pushing them both into yet another orgasm.

This was all too much for Eric. Dick so tight it felt like it'd split, he gasped and yanked it from the warm wet hold of Joy's vagina. With a shudder, he shoved it between Taniese's lips and had to fight a scream as she promptly sucked his soul out. Licking and slurping, she took every last drop. He sent wave after wave between her lips and down her throat, and she drank and swallowed it all, noisily and greedily.

At last, all three collapsed in a wet heap on the floor. Eric fell back, his arm across his eyes, then sat up and smacked Taniese on her ass.

"I'ma have to give it to you, shorty," he said, his voice clouded with the sleepy swells of satisfaction. "You definitely picked a winner."

"I told you, didn't I?" She stood, stretching languidly, body glistening in the light. Passing him on her way to the kitchen, she leaned down and kissed him on the lips. "And am I ever wrong?" She laughed and scampered off as he rose up to pop her playfully.

"Man, don't even get me started." He was about to say more, but found himself suddenly stuck when he felt Joy's lips wrap around his dick. Surprising herself, she'd found a well of sexual reserves she didn't realize she had. Body hot, temp raised, mouth and pussy wet, she was ready for another round, rounds, all and everything the night had to offer.

"After all of that," Eric thought to himself with mild astonishment, "she's already ready to go again?" He sighed and closed his eyes as he felt her lips work their magic, bringing him back to full, pulsing life.

"You win this round, shorty," he said with a sigh and a smile. "You do win this round..."